LUCIE PAYE's debut novel *Les coeurs inquiets* was published to critical acclaim during the first lockdown in France in March 2020, in Éditions Gallimard's prestigious Collection Blanche. Further to studies at the École du Louvre, she published several works on garden history before a career in arts management. She lived in California for several years and now lives in London, with her two children.

NATASHA LEHRER is an award-winning journalist and translator, and laureate of the Scott Moncrieff Prize for her co-translation of Nathalie Léger's *Suite for Barbara Loden*. Her other translations include *Journey to the Land of the Real* by Victor Segalen, *Memories of Low Tide* by Chantal Thomas and *Consent* by Vanessa Springora.

ABSENCE

Lucie Paye

Translated from the French
by Natasha Lehrer

Les Fugitives

Absence

I saw the angel in the marble and carved until I set him free.

MICHELANGELO BUONARROTI

The heart shuts,
The sea slides back,
The mirrors are sheeted.

SYLVIA PLATH
'Contusion', *Ariel*

He - Prologue

The painting frothed under his brushstrokes. The sea,
its mottled green hues rippling in the wind, a thick
deposit swirling in the currents. Under his pressure,
the cliff opened onto an image: a garden. He beat a path
through, blind and sighted all at once. The grain of the
canvas, thick paint squeezed from the tubes, turning
into bark, stem, grass, leaf, moss. In the centre of the
garden stood a figure. There had never been one in his
landscapes before. At first he thought it was a play of
the light, the afterimage of a ray of sunshine through
the trees, but then it began to take shape: a woman was
walking towards him. The shadows of the vegetation
swathed her now in a dappled cloak. Her face, framed
by long hair, was half-hidden by the curve of a palm
frond. Her hand was raised to push it aside, but the
movement, suspended in mid-air, masked her eyes. He
guessed at her mouth. He followed the line of her lips.
Impatience made him clumsy. He knew that this was
only the beginning. The moment would come when
these lips would open to whisper their secret to him.
He knew her eyes would, in due course, emerge from
the shadows. Then, perhaps, he might find what he was
looking for.

She – Prologue

When I'm dreaming, when I'm awake, alone, in company, on a terrace, in a garden, I never stop seeing you. There before me, fleetingly alive, before reality is restored and steals you away again. I have fought to find you with every fibre of my being. Hope has kept me alive. A thousand mornings I have woken up convinced today would be the day. A thousand times my heart has leapt, thinking I had caught a glimpse of you. A thousand times I have gone to bed, wanting to believe that tomorrow would be the day I would see you again. I have embalmed the tiniest detail of every memory I have of you. I do sometimes lose heart. I worry I won't recognise you: your forehead, your nose, your mouth. Your lovely forehead, snub nose, rosebud mouth, pretty chin... *Mon tout amour*. But your eyes – no, they won't have changed. Your eyes – I'd recognise them anywhere.

He

He pushed open the door of the gallery with effort. He nearly hadn't come. Thought of finding some excuse at the last minute. Or not even bothering with an excuse. Of staying in the studio to paint, forgetting the world, even as it persisted in turning. It felt as if the exhibition had been just yesterday. Several months had passed. The gallery seemed larger than before.

Marc crossed the room with his easy stride and wide smile, and greeted him ebulliently. He acknowledged the warmth of the welcome with embarrassment, as though it were an undeserved gift.

'Shall we go into my office? Can I get you a coffee?'

'Yes. Thank you.'

'Make yourself at home. I'll be right back.' Marc disappeared.

He remained on his feet, hesitated to sit down. The imposing armchair Marc had gestured him towards glowered at him. Eventually, resolutely, he sat down on the edge of the chair, then he leaned back, then forward again. He decided not to put his arms on the armrests, instead he placed his hands on his thighs. The paint marks on his hands were like scars that had spread onto his jeans. It hadn't occurred to him to change clothes. He looked around the room as if seeing it for the first time: neatly ordered catalogues, a shiny new computer, an elegant pen making a diagonal black line on a white sheet of paper. His gaze skidded, as if unable to attach itself to the sleek, angular, glossy surfaces.

Marc reappeared and handed him a perfectly white porcelain cup. With his broad smile, he sat down behind his desk.

'It's good to see you. How's things?'

'Fine.'

Marc asked him questions about his life, his health, his days – small talk. He waited, tense, his mind both empty and frantically occupied with what was to come.

'I hope you do more than just work!'

'Yes, kind of.'

'Are you happy with what you're doing?'

Here was the invitation to emerge from the wings. But he froze at the word 'happy', a word that didn't suit him and held him back from answering. Marc pressed him:

'I can pop by and take a look one of these days, if you like.'

'I'd rather not. Not yet.'

Marc picked up the black and gold pen and began toying with it.

'Okay then. But would you like to have a chat anyway?'

'Why not.'

What was there to say?

'Are you working on any new paintings?'

'Yes.'

'And?'

The cup hovered at Marc's lips. No answer was forth-coming, so the cup was emptied in a single gulp then pushed to the edge of the desk, as one might dispose of one idea to make room for the next.

'Do you remember the collector who bought the view of the garden with the little pond? A tall brunette, quite good-looking, with a bit of a lisp?'

He did indeed remember the painting, but not the woman.

'She's been asking me if you have any similar pieces. One of her friends is interested. I don't know the friend, but if you ask me, this is an opportunity not to be missed. Do you have anything you could show her?'

'I don't think so.'

'The lady in question is a collector as well; she's got a very good eye, according to her friend. I'm quite willing to believe that's the case, given her interest in your work.'

He forced himself to smile, to thank Marc for his partiality.

'I'll have to think about it.'

'She's not asking for the moon, don't worry. It doesn't need to be new. I thought you could just show them whatever you have stashed away. They suggested coming by the studio. A short visit. They'd love to see how you work: a glimpse into the artist's life.'

He fixed his gaze on Marc: his affable air, his solid physique framed by the black leather armchair, cut off at the waist by the smooth plane of the desk. If he could have drawn the gallerist just then it would have been a candid portrait.

'I'm sorry, Marc, no. I've got nothing to show them.'

'Come on, man, just this once, you'll make them so happy. The hoary old fantasy of bohemian life. You understand that! A short visit, no fuss, they'll be in heaven.'

'No, really. I can't. I'm sorry.'

He wanted to explain, fumbled for the words, but came up with nothing. He looked away, through the window. People walked past on the other side of the glass, soundless. The sun leaked a pale-yellow square onto the wall opposite. It shattered as a woman walked through it. He'd have liked the bubble he was trapped inside to shatter too. He felt a sharp twinge of pain in his temple. He raised his hand to it. Marc stood up and took a few fretful steps across the small room.

'Alright, never mind. We'll do it another way.' He sat down again. 'You don't want anyone to come to the studio, I get that... but tell me just one thing: are you working on anything? I'm getting to know you now.'

Marc's eyes probed his own. 'It doesn't have to be finished; if there's anything you're not sure about we can even talk about that.'

He had to say it, now, very quickly.

'Yes, there is something; but I'm really not sure.'

Marc's expression urged him on.

'The thing is, I've painted a woman. I mean, she painted herself. Just a sketch.' He couldn't stop now. 'She just appeared in the painting. Only one painting.' He was rushing ahead of himself, the gradient spooked him, he wanted to slow down. 'Not really her face. Just her silhouette, her outline.' His voice sounded far away as he went on, 'I'd like to follow her.'

'A woman?'

He didn't want Marc to get the wrong end of the stick. Absolutely not. But what else could he say? Even he didn't know where she'd appeared from, or why, or who she was. The coffee in the cup he was holding was cold. He took a sip. Marc repeated, 'A woman?'

The bitterness of the coffee made his tongue fur up. 'You think I'm on the wrong track?'

Marc raised an eyebrow.

'Wrong track? I have no idea.'

But who else would know? How could he explain it to Marc? Explain what? He needed to get all these fragments, these little scraps of images floating around his head, to fuse together somehow.

'If it makes you feel any better, you know you don't need to change direction right now. People like your style. You're only just beginning to build a body of work. You can afford to keep going at your own pace. Your landscapes are wonderful. But of course if you have a glimmering of something else... Are you sure you don't want me to come and take a look?'

Keep moving forward, but don't trip up. Create, but don't fabricate. He was caught in a vice.

'Maybe. Let me think about it. I'll let you know.'

Marc stood up again. Was the interview over already?

'I've got something to say to you as well.' Marc stood there, one hand on the bookcase with its neat stack of catalogues.

'What would you say to an exhibition in September?'

He wasn't sure he'd heard right.

'An exhibition?'

'Yes, your second.'

Silence.

'I don't know.'

'Now to September gives you nine months. That's enough, no?'

Nine months? His stomach clenched.

'Do I have to tell you straight away?'

'Of course not. It can wait till next week. Fifteen paintings, that's all. It'll help if you have a deadline, you'll see.'

He didn't know what to say; he said nothing. Marc looked at his watch.

'Alright. I hope you'll think about it. Remember, I'm here if you need any advice. You can call me whenever.'

Marc opened the door.

'You'll have to forgive me, I'm not throwing you out, but I have a lunch appointment. With a woman. I can't paint her, so I've invited her out to lunch instead. It's the best I can do!'

She

Mon tout amour,
I have just learnt that I am very ill. I am not going to
get better. The doctor tried to spare me the details,
but it was obvious. My days are numbered. In all
honesty, they always were; it's simply that now I know
I have even fewer ahead of me than I had imagined. A
few months, a year at most.

The time has come for regrets. I only have one. All
these years I have yearned for one thing, had but one
wish, and now I'm beginning to realise that I shall
die without it being granted. I am not afraid of dying,
but I am furious that it's my fate to be deprived of the
time I need to find you.

That is why I've decided to write to you. I've
always dismissed the idea, but now I see it as a way
of continuing to hope even beyond the grave. It's
only human nature. Is it awfully egotistical of me?
Talking to you after I'm dead is like offering a gift and
snatching it back in the same movement. I imagine
you with this letter in your hand. It's not that I want
you to suffer. I don't want you to rail against fate. I
don't want to bequeath you anger or hate. Quite the
opposite.

He

He sat on a stool at the studio worktable, cluttered with a jumble of pots, tubes, pencils and brushes. His drawings were lifeless. He hadn't been able to pick up a paintbrush all day. What a waste of a day. He put down his pencil. The floor was littered with soulless sketches. He began tinkering mindlessly with a box cutter, making notches in the wooden tabletop. Marc's ultimatum loomed over him: an exhibition in September. The syllables pounded repeatedly in his head. He couldn't do it. That first exhibition had been no more than a fluke. Marc, on holiday in Mauritius, spotted his work in the hotel where he was showing his paintings. After that, everything else had happened so fast. No time to take it all in. It was meaningless. An accident.

And yet, an exhibition, in Paris, what more could one ask for? Recognition. But in whose eyes? And what if it didn't mean anything? If it didn't really count? He was close to thinking that. All those island landscapes. And now? He had to start all over again. Why not paint Paris? He couldn't. He couldn't see anything there. Only hollow images. Maybe the ones of Mauritius were hollow too. And to think that he'd sold them! Now he couldn't destroy them. It was too late. He pressed the box cutter deeper into the flesh of the table.

Everything had been easier in Port-Louis. He'd been safe there. The vegetation was so overgrown that daylight barely pierced the windows. He painted under an electric bulb. He could hear the sea. He still heard it at night, high above the apartment buildings, chatting with the wind. The sea around his island. At the beginning, he didn't know. He had to spend hours on the beach, in gardens, fields, the forest, to capture the details. He laboured like a carthorse on his compositions. But soon he was going out less. He didn't need to anymore. The landscapes became his. His island lived within him, flowed from him onto the canvas. At last he was grasping something impalpable. He remembered these paintings in legato, each one giving birth to the next. He was a gaping mouth. Matter flooded out of him. Until Paris. Until now when nothing came out anymore. Nothing was right. No matter how hard he tried, no matter how much he forced the paint onto the canvas. He was fumbling, shuffling, going round in circles. He was washed up, spent, on a deserted beach. A carcass filled with vast black emptiness.

He stared at the pile of sketches, the ripped-apart sketch books, the overflowing ashtray, the scattering of ash, in his dogged determination to find something. The sequel. He'd wanted to keep going on the same track. In vain. An illusion. He swivelled on the stool. He looked around the studio: the plaster, the wooden floor, the boards, the easel, the canvases turned to face the wall. He saw them from behind, their backs, the ghostly skin divided into four by the crossbar of the stretcher. Each time he finished one, he would slam its face against a wall of the room. He didn't want to look at them. If he did, he wouldn't be able to carry on. They would thwart him. Like when his father used to stand behind him and watch him painting, the way his hand would start to tremble.

It was Marc who'd suggested he come and live in Paris. And he'd been feeling he needed a change anyway. A combination of circumstances. He'd grabbed the opportunity. At what point exactly did he make up his mind? He couldn't remember. He couldn't remember deciding. It was more of an impulse. An intuition. On top of the death of his father. Centuries ago. He counted. Not even a year in fact. Gone in an instant. Heart attack. Dropped dead. His body on the tiled floor of the terrace, burnt by the sun. He remembered the disbelief. A helpless rage, as if something had been stolen from him. Something that was rightly his. Something he was owed. He couldn't have said what. It wasn't his father. He wouldn't miss him. When he was little, he would sometimes lie in bed and imagine him dead. He'd wake up and his father wouldn't be there, ever again. He'd have been in a car crash or struck by lightning. And then his breathing would slow, his muscles would relax, and at last he would fall asleep. Sometimes, afterwards, he'd dream of his mother, emerging from the water, seaweed braided in her hair. She'd embrace him, then take his hand and together they would wade into the sweet-smelling ocean. They would swim, side by side, up to the horizon where she lived.

He'd like to see it all again, but his memories were fading, like a dreamscape, now that he lived in Paris, as if it wasn't he who had lived that other life. The succession of events had been so rapid: his father's death, the sale of the house, Marc, who had organised the exhibition and suggested he come to France, the lease on his apartment terminated, his studio emptied. Then Paris: the cramped apartment where he lived and painted, the private view, meeting Ariane, and now Marc pushing him even more. He shivered. A cold draught blew through the ill-fitting window frame. He refused to turn up the heating because of the bill. What an idiotic thing to worry about. He remembered the heat in Mauritius. He dug another notch in the plywood, shaped like a wave.

The eve of his departure, his last night, he had gone for a walk on the beach. No question of farewells. He didn't like them. His routine was to take a walk along the shore after a day of shadowboxing with paint. That evening it was already dark, the moon hung in the sky. He walked along the edge of the water. His bare feet looked like dark crabs. As the waves danced, he walked with a heavy syncopated tread. Something was changing, definitively. He was an interloper to everything: the splash of the stars, their pale wash against the inky sky, the rustle of the casuarina trees, the stifling, perfumed heat. He had become a foreign body in this world teeming with life. He could describe the elements without thinking, like speaking his mother tongue, but from now on they would never signify anything ever again. That evening, his island was no longer the same. His confidante, his warm-bellied consoler, had abandoned him. Whenever his father's implacable coldness used to make him cry, he would run and hide, spit his rage into the island's lap. The rocky inlets were kind, the arms of the frangipani gentle, the waves of the lagoon caressing. He had thought it was he who was abandoning the island, but really it was the island who had abandoned him.

He got up and went to the bathroom, reached into the shower, and turned on the hot tap. It always took a while for the water to heat up. He looked at himself in the mirror, at the black smudges of charcoal on his face. Pathetic. He undressed, mechanically. He was thinking about the woman. Soon the tiny room was engulfed in a dense, steamy fug. Despite the shower curtain, a puddle was forming on the floor. He used his foot to push the bathmat closer to contain it. He got into the shower and banged his funny bone on the soap holder. A tiny shock ran down his arm. He ignored it. The heat relaxed his muscles. He stood there, head under the spray, eyes closed, water flowing into his mouth. He pictured the canvas again. Yes, there was this painting. This woman. He wanted to see her face, to push her hand away, but something was holding him back.

Dried off and dressed, he looked at his watch: it was past four already. He was hungry. He grabbed his sketchbook, pencil and jacket and left. Out in the street, the cold air hit his face. His wet hair froze. He pulled up his collar. A day as grey as pencil lead. His thoughts were still on the studio floor, stuck to the scraps of sketches, like a skin he couldn't quite shed. He quickened his pace. He'd forgotten that out on the street life went on. He stared with astonishment at people walking, shopping, eating, with family, friends, colleagues. He needed to get out more. He noticed people glancing at him. He must look like a bear. He didn't care. He didn't owe anyone anything.

He went into the café on the corner of the street and

was immediately enveloped in the noise and the bustle. The owner greeted him briefly, scowling: one of those days, you know. He ordered a sandwich and took a seat at his usual table by the window.

He sat quite still for a moment, back bowed, head in hand. Only his finger unthinkingly traced the edge of the table where the Formica joined. He absorbed the music in the café. He began to warm up. He must have been a Parisian in a former existence. The fact that he'd lived in this city for the first three years of his life wasn't enough to explain the relief he felt just then. Like coming back to life. He had Paris in his veins, a transfusion.

A laugh caused him to lift his head. At the next table, two schoolgirls were chatting. The one in his line of sight had a face that was round and plump. She kept tucking a lock of blonde hair behind her ear. Her eyes crinkled when she laughed. She had a dimple in the hollow of her left cheek. He took the pencil from his pocket, opened his sketchbook, and dashed off a likeness in a few brief strokes. She caught his eye and smiled. Women often smiled at him. He turned his attention to the passers-by in the street. He drew them too. A woman, weighed down with shopping, waiting to cross, a stooped old man, a vagrant on a bench, people queuing for the bus, a delivery man, a postman, a saleswoman smoking outside the shoe shop, two friends saying goodbye to each other.

He had always drawn. In the silent house. He and his father spoke no more to each other than necessary. Outside, the garden rustled and chirped, alive with birds, rain and wind. His father was busy with other things. He drew. On paper he could do what he wanted. He went to the zoo multiple times a day to see animals that didn't exist. He climbed crooked mountains. He set sail and drifted around crimson suns. He opened the doors to multicoloured houses. His mother was inside. Those drawings he hid. He drew the island too, just as it was, without changing anything. It was so beautiful, the water in the air, the crazy sunshine, the tousled coronet of the casuarina trees, the waves carved from crystal, the red crepe of the hibiscus flowers, the scented pearls of the cinnamon tree, the grains of sand tattooed on his skin.

The waiter put down a sandwich in front of him. The bistro came back into focus. He ate greedily, then ordered a coffee and went back to studying the passers-by. There wasn't time for them to take shape properly. He made snatched sketches. Just outlines really, some key element. He'd always enjoyed this exercise. Snaring a soul with the stroke of a pencil. At school he used to sketch his teachers and classmates. It was like stealing a little bit of them, without them knowing, and slipping it inside his drawing. He thought back to the pickpocket who'd stolen his wallet the first week he was in Paris. He'd been hopping mad. The stupid little shit. But what he did was the same thing, in a way.

It was easy. He could look at someone's external appearance and effortlessly it became lines, confident and true. Except that inside himself everything was murky. Inside he was an amorphous mush. He knew the woman in the painting dwelled in there, but he couldn't work out how to see her. Perhaps he should find a real woman to model her. That would be easier. Marc would be happy. But he couldn't do it. That would be cheating. And lying. He sensed a fine thread between his fingers, unspooling into the darkness. He determined to grasp and pull it until he reached the very end.

'Are you drawing?'

He started. The baby-faced schoolgirl had sat down in front of him.

'No, I'm threading beads.'

She laughed. She smelled of cheap perfume.

'Can I see?'

'No.' He closed his sketchbook.

'Are you an artist?'

'If you like.'

Her teeth were white. They looked like milk teeth. Her smile was a little asinine.

'Are you looking for models?'

'No.'

Her face fell.

'Shame for you then,' she said. He didn't react, but she stayed where she sat. 'Because me and my friend could model for you. We've done it before. For a photographer.'

That was enough.

'I just said I don't use models.'

He got up, gathered his pencil and sketchbook, and went to pay at the counter. Outside in the street he wondered who was more laughable, the girl or him.

She

I feel a bit of a fool writing to you like this. I always want to talk to you, and yet all of a sudden I have no idea what to tell you. A kind of shyness. I want to ask you a thousand questions, not talk about myself. Writing to you is a way of imagining you answering me. What did life have in store for you? How did it turn out? Such big questions, and so many of them. It's almost absurd. 'The absurd is the essential concept and the first truth.' Camus said that, I think. It's hard to accept. I have so many questions gnawing at me. Now I'm beginning to understand that I shall never have any answers. Instead I shall try to give you some, my dearest, my one true love.

He

An idea came to him: to retrace his steps. That's what he'd do. Go back to the crossroad, to the moment when the woman first appeared. The jolt of shock. The mechanism of his earlier paintings was broken. He'd been roused from slumber by the woman in the forsaken garden. He sensed something living, some miniscule thing, barely perceptible, stirring in him. Deep within, it was beginning to germinate. It would take time. Yes, that was it, he'd start again with this painting. To escape this blind alley, he'd go back to the moment when the woman appeared. Perhaps then something would happen.

He took a large sheet of cartridge paper and clipped it to the easel, then raised the support bar. He wanted to draw standing up, like a fighter. He attacked the vegetation: sloping palm fronds, stiff branches. The charcoal crumbled against the paper: little showers of black dust spilled over the creamy grain. The feel of the leaves, a flat, blurred plane of pigment under his fingers. Black flowers, unfurling before him in colour. Or the opposite: he saw them as black but really they were in colour, he couldn't tell the difference anymore. The breeze made the light dance. Fragrance bloomed in the humid air. In a fold, shadows began to burrow.

The phone rang. He stopped drawing, hesitated, then let it go through to the answering machine. He heard Ariane's low, liquid voice:

'It's me. Are you there?' Silence. Her breath. 'Are you alright?' Another silence, then other words, a little softer. 'I miss you. Can we see each other?' Then, more assertive: 'Call me.' Her breath hung on the line.

He made a slight movement. Click. She'd hung up. The answering machine squeaked then fell silent. On the easel, his drawing towered over him. Now he saw the silhouette, nestled in the vegetation. Yes, he could see her again. This time she wasn't standing; she sat, half turned away, a book open on her lap. She wasn't reading though. Her head was turned towards him. Her features were blurred. He grabbed the charcoal. Traced lines, the oval of her face, the movement of her neck, the twist of her torso. He travelled down her arms to meet her hands. Her wrist was loose, but her fingers were tensed, to keep the book from slipping from their grasp. They were at rest, but alert. She wasn't relaxed. And her face? Her mouth? Her expression? He continued drawing, then rubbing with the flat of his fist. He saw nothing, nothing at all. He closed his eyes for a long moment. This was his solution whenever he went blind; in the darkness, he regained his sight. But this time there was nothing. Just the emptiness inside him. Ariane's words came and lodged there: 'I miss you.'

He took a new sheet of paper. He roughly drew some eyes, rubbed them, drew over them again. It was hopeless. They were dead. They were wrong. He tried again. The sheet filled with eyes. None of them were right. He felt a cramp the length of his forearm, but he refused to stop. He would try the mouth instead. He had captured it in the first painting, graceful and shy. This time she was about to speak. He wanted to hear her. This mouth would speak today. His fingers seized up. He swapped the charcoal to his other hand. He didn't care if it was wobbly. He would capture her with his left hand if he had to. He would force her. Make her reveal herself, whatever it took. It was all he could think about. It was all he could do. He bit his own lip until it bled. This mouth was hers. Her lips. He stopped blinking. He couldn't take his eyes off her for an instant. This mouth, under his fingers, drawn over and over, a thousand times, never right, never captured, never there. Silent as the grave. A voiceless mouth. Empty eyes. An elusive face. His vision grew blurred. Fury strained his muscles. He could have screamed. He slammed the board with his fist and sent it spinning. The easel collapsed with it and hit the ground with a loud crash. He stared at his failure, the spoiled cartridge paper crushed beneath the board, his useless, blackened hands. He wiped them on his face. War paint. He wasn't giving up, he was just catching his breath.

He sat on the radiator and leaned against the window. The metallic warmth contrasted with the chill of the glass at his back. He lit a cigarette. His feet trampled the pencilled debris of the previous days. All rejected. A crowd of women. A mocking crowd of anonymous women. The one he was looking for was hiding somewhere. He let his head fall back against the cold windowpane. It was an obstacle course. If he fell he would have to pick himself up again, not allow himself to slow down. A long-distance race. He was going to fill the sheets of paper with faces. He would keep moving. He wouldn't stop until he crossed the finish line. That face, yes, that face, he would find it eventually. He would keep drawing, over and over again. Who was this woman? He could swear she wasn't here, and yet he still couldn't actually picture her.

When he finished his cigarette, he sat down at the table and took a pencil from a jar. He opened a sketchbook. He planted the pencil lead in the centre of the page like the point of a knife. Ready to rip through the veil. He pressed harder. His fingers shook. Pain shot through his wrist. He dropped the pencil. He stared at the blank paper. The tiny grey mark made by the pencil lead. He felt his pulse beating in his right temple. The beginning of headache.

Marc's ultimatum. Fifteen paintings. And he was like a rotten piece of fruit. Eaten away from the inside. The vultures had come back to circle him. The landscapes he had carried on painting. Dumbly, like a beast, like an ant. To monetise relics of the past? He couldn't bear it. The whiteness of the paper burnt his eyes. He looked away. He began kicking, again and again, faster and faster, making the stool he sat on spin. He made himself dizzy. He spun round and round, tailed by the puppet waving from the floor: his shadow.

Abruptly he stopped. His head was throbbing with pain. He clenched his fists. He still had an urge to fight, to wrestle. He stood up and crossed the short distance separating him from the stretchered canvases. He began turning them round. His lousy paintings. One by one. He displayed them without ceremony. Against the walls, against the window, on the bed. The studio had fallen dark. He switched on the light. The electric light struck the paintings brashly. He liked that. He dragged the stool into the centre of the room and sat down to study them.

They stood upright around him under the harsh ceiling light. It was up to him now to judge them. He alone was judge. Judge and master. He dispelled all memory of making them, pushed away the physicality of the recollection. They were detached from him now. He took his time, took the time to penetrate each one. He let his eyes wander over them. They tried to seduce him. He might almost have allowed himself to be seduced, if it hadn't been for the shocked realisation that he had painted all this. Why? The evidence was taking shape, weighty as a punishment. All for nothing, that was the verdict. There was nothing in these paintings. They were vain. They were dumb. Entertainment. Empty, venal assembly-line work. None of it was worth a thing. And yet he'd believed in it while he was doing it. Sometimes he'd even thought it was quite good. What a joke. Now he saw them finished, their lies were blindingly obvious.

He covered his face with his hands. He couldn't bear to look at them anymore. But he could still sense them, surrounding him, all these imposters with their eyes fixed on him. They tormented him. He could barely breathe. Marc must be mad. He couldn't possibly have another exhibition, not in September, not with these paintings. It was all wrong. He picked up the box cutter. He began with the largest. One by one, in a frenzy, he began to slice into them. He ripped their supple flesh, slashed them to ribbons. The big ones first, then the rest. All of them. He was the vulture, he was the scavenger. His visions: rotten carcasses. Before long there was nothing left but flaps of skin dangling off wooden skeletons. He put down his weapon. He felt dizzy. He steadied himself against the table. His fingers were bloody. He'd cut his left hand. He picked up a rag and pressed it against the wound.

He listened to his hacking breaths. There was one left. Only one. It stood a little away from the others. He put down the rag, ignoring the blood as it began flowing again. He dragged her roughly to the middle of the room. The woman. He looked her full in the face. She had come unbidden. In the shadows, the perfumed air, the breeze and the clammy heat. He stared hard at her. He wasn't going to let her go. She had lifted a hand to move the foliage aside. The enveloping silence was suddenly unbearable. He said aloud, 'Come.' The figure didn't move. He said it again, louder: 'Come.' He put out an arm to touch the canvas. The blood left a red mark. His hand was shaking. His decision was made.

He picked up the phone and dialled Marc's number. No answer. A voice invited him to leave a message. 'Marc, it's me. You can come over.' He hung up. The only thing that mattered was this woman.

She

I went to see the Hopper retrospective yesterday. If
only you could have seen those figures, the solitude,
the absolute silence amid the din. Time stood still
in the gallery. I could feel the stillness of the air,
the invisible walls, the sense of people being at
one remove from others and from themselves, the
emptiness at the heart of things, so many unfulfilled
expectations.

There was *Nighthawks*, of course, night owls sitting
at the counter of a diner, behind glass. Have you
ever noticed the thick, cheerless glass we're always
knocking against? We see other people only as an
image.

In the middle of the exhibition, I had the familiar
prickling sensation of seeing you. In the crowd, a few
steps away from me, stood a young man looking at
a painting. I recognised the texture of his hair; I'd
kissed his body; I knew the sweetness of his breath.
He had his back to me, so I couldn't see his face. I
didn't need to. There you were. But then, too quickly,
as always, reason took over. I shook off the familiar
illusion and moved away before the stranger could
turn his head, to avoid the pain of acknowledging that
it wasn't you.

But if our paths were ever to cross in real life, would
we recognise each other? Does it really exist, this
unbreakable thread that I want to believe in? If fate

were ever to bring us face to face, would I know it was you? My love, amaranthine, light years after we were torn apart.

He

He didn't know what to do with his hands, so he thrust them into his pockets. Marc had blown into the studio like a gale, with his tailored blazer and flawless ski tan. He could still feel the pressure of his embrace on his back and cheek. If he were to paint Marc it would have to be in acrylics, with no shadow. Even here, among the paint stains, the pentimenti, the doubts, the gallerist looked immaculate. Indestructible amid the chaos.

He'd done his best to cover up the slashed paintings, but Marc spotted them right away and gave a whistle of ironic admiration.

'Goodness me. Looks like you've been settling a few scores.'

He offered him coffee by way of a response. Marc glanced at the coffee pot. It was white, beneath the dried paint and coffee stains.

'No, thank you. I'm trying to cut back on caffeine.'

Marc stood in front of the easel and without a word began to study it. Time stood still. He waited. He waited for Marc to say something. He fumbled for his cigarettes. They weren't in his pockets. He couldn't see them. He crossed the room and found them in his jacket hanging on the coat rack. Marc hadn't moved. Just one cigarette left. He lit it, screwed up the packet and tossed it towards the wastepaper basket, which he missed. When Marc spoke again he almost jumped.

'Why this woman?'

A piece of charcoal lay on the floor. He crushed it beneath his heel.

'I don't know.'

'Did you have a model?'

'No.'

'So who is she?'

He shrugged. He'd never asked himself the question. It was of no importance. Marc remained standing in front of the painting. The light sculpted his face. The vein on his forehead, the crook of his nose, the dimple in his chin. Mentally he followed the contour of Marc's designer stubble, its chiselled definition, the slight curve of his jawline.

'Are you still with Ariane?' asked Marc.

'Sort of.'

He'd met Ariane through Marc, indirectly. She wrote catalogue copy for the gallery. She came to his private view. They talked that evening for quite a while. It was like a cool breeze that took the edge off the stultifying airlessness of the party. A few days later they met up again for a drink. A relationship began to develop. After a while he took a step back, for fear of committing to something he couldn't deliver, but Ariane had managed to talk him round, without making any demands.

'Have you met someone else?'

'No, no.'

Marc's expression forced an explanation.

'Listen, Marc. I honestly don't know who this woman is.' He spoke slowly and clearly, as though to someone who was hard of hearing. Smoke emerged before the words. 'She doesn't exist. Except in the painting. What she's come for, I have no idea.' He drew slowly on his cigarette. 'All I know is that I want to carry on.' A long exhalation, accompanied by hazy white whorls. 'I want to follow her. I want to talk about her. It's got nothing to do with Ariane or anything else.' He turned his head towards the window to avoid Marc's gaze. Otherwise his words would have got stuck in his throat. Ash dropped from his cigarette. The grey cinders made a tiny little volcanic mound on the floor.

'I need to know what you think.' He made one last attempt. 'You have to tell me if it's sound, if it's going to work.'

There, he'd said it. Now he waited for Marc to offer him something tangible, a life jacket. He stared out at the apartments on the other side of the courtyard. Marc came and put a hand on his shoulder.

'It's not up to me to decide. Even if I wanted to, I couldn't. All I can say is I can see something of you in this painting. And that's what matters. That's what interests me.'

Deep down, what more did he expect?

'So you think I should keep going with it?'

Marc turned back to look at the painting.

'Yes. As long as it's not just a passing whim. If you feel it's serious, you must carry on. Paint this woman. It doesn't matter who it is. We'll find out later. Or not.'

He accompanied Marc down the stairs and out onto the street. He watched him climb into a taxi, then walked round the corner to the bureau de tabac. The woman behind the counter greeted him with a smile she reserved for regulars. She asked him something, but her words were drowned out by the clamour of a passing scooter. He responded with a nod; he had no idea what she'd said. He noticed she had gone from a blonde to a redhead, and that her face looked different as a result. He paid and left. He sat down on the first bench he came to and lit a cigarette, but the wind was glacial and he didn't sit for long.

Inside the building's hallway he checked his mailbox. There was some junk mail and a postcard. *The Snake Charmer*, by Rousseau. He knew it only from reproductions. A shadow rather than a woman, surrounded by untamed vegetation. On the back, in her fine, elegant hand, Ariane had written:

Do you, false captive of this foliage, know
how these thin boughs eat up the outer glow,
how secrets dazzle though my eyes are closed.

My love will always recommence.
Paul Valéry makes me think of you.

She'd sent him a painting of a woman. Marc must have told her. That was when he remembered her message on the answering machine. He'd forgotten to call her back. When had he last checked his mailbox? The card could have been sitting there for days.

He climbed the stairs to the apartment. It stank of oil. He barely noticed it anymore except when he walked in the door, then he forgot all about it. He went straight over to the phone and dialled Ariane's number. She answered immediately. Her voice was like a stream of crystal. She didn't take him to task, just asked him a few questions. 'Yes.' He had received her postcard. He thanked her. 'Yes.' Dinner the following evening would be nice. 'Okay.' At the restaurant downstairs from her apartment.

As they talked, his eyes were fixed on the broad slats of the wooden floor. They were splattered with blobs of dried paint. He knew their forms by heart. There was the dog, the swan, the smashed-up car. He spotted a new mark. It looked like the silhouette of a pregnant woman.

'See you tomorrow then?'

'Yes, see you tomorrow.'

He hung up, took the pencil from his pocket, and crouched down to draw round the shape. He emphasised the curve of the belly. He straightened up and contemplated it and then rubbed the sole of his shoe up and down, smudging the outline. He hung up his jacket and scarf and sat down at the worktable. What to make of Marc's approval?

Absentmindedly, he picked up the nearest sketchbook. He flicked through the pages and came to the figures he'd drawn at the café the other day. He'd forgotten all about them. Idly he began reworking them. Ariane's voice came back to him. 'See you tomorrow then?' She always enunciated her words quietly and clearly. She had this way of pushing without nagging. How long had it been since she'd last come over? They almost always saw each other at her apartment. She never said 'the studio', she said 'the lair'. It was true that it wasn't ideal for a couple. But it wasn't supposed to be. He lived and worked in one room. He shared his life with his paintings, with trestle tables, tubes, cans of paint and brushes. Books piled up on the floor alongside overloaded shelves. He slept on a mattress in the corner. Often, after hours of painting, he'd collapse on it without even crawling beneath the sheets. He liked how the distance between his work and his life had become infinitesimal. It made painting like breathing. He painted, dreaming, while he slept. He dreamed, awake, while he painted. The hours moulded perfectly to the contours of his labour. He got lost in it. 'Your painting is my rival,' he remembered Ariane once saying. He sketched her profile. Then he surrounded her with the foliage of a burgeoning garden.

As night fell, he could no longer see to draw. He got up and walked over to the window, treading on pieces of paper strewn across the floor. Dusk consumed the courtyard and studio. He hadn't noticed it was getting dark. A grey-yellow veil floated over the glowing lights of the city. He lit a cigarette. A gust of cold air insinuated itself through the window frame. The lights in the windows of the building opposite formed a haphazard grid. People, moving around. He could spend hours watching this silent film: snippets stolen from the reels of other people's lives by the scissors of chance.

In the ten months he'd been living there, he had grown familiar with his neighbours' habits. It was a bit like the game at the café, but over time. On the first floor lived an elderly woman. She moved in slow motion, very carefully, like an old monk. There was a family on the second floor: kids coming and going, a father who got home late, a mother performing the same daily tasks on a loop, brunches and dinners with friends at the weekend. Shiny snapshots. He felt very distant from that kind of life. His own was lacklustre. On the upper floors the apartments were smaller.

People randomly materialised and disappeared: students cramming for exams, a cleaning woman at work, her phone wedged between her ear and shoulder, a man behind a huge computer screen, a couple having sex in front of a flickering television. And then, among them, this woman. At least fifty, maybe older. It was hard to tell. She was beautiful. That was the first, inane, thought he'd had about her. For lack of a better word. Because he was sensitive to beauty, a certain kind of beauty.

That evening she was sitting at her desk. She usually was. She was writing. The two windows he could see looked into her bedroom. He saw the bed through the window on the right; through the one on the left, the desk against the wall. Between the two, in the part that escaped his view, there may have been a door. It wasn't a large room. The slats of the parquet floor disappeared towards the back in brief converging lines.

He crushed out his cigarette and went over to the cupboard where he kept jackets, tools, an ironing board, a sleeping bag. He rummaged through the clutter until he found a pair of binoculars. Then he turned off the light and went to sit in the armchair by the long window. He adjusted the focus. The woman's head appeared in the circular field of vision.

This was the first time he had ever done anything like this. He'd never seen her in close-up before. Once again, he couldn't help thinking how beautiful she was. He studied her profile. Her thick hair, spun through with a few grey hairs, was held back with a clip. He studied the dome of her forehead, her straight, slightly prominent nose, her sensual mouth. Mentally he traced its contour. Her lips were parted. As she wrote, they seemed to quiver. He imagined her breath escaping. He wanted to see her hand holding the pen, even the shape of her words, but there was something in the way. It was an antique candlestick. An object from another era. Maybe she enjoyed browsing flea markets early in the morning when there were still bargains to be had, or perhaps it was a family heirloom. He followed the metal ring. A flickering, dancing flame: though the bedroom was brightly lit, a candle was burning, melting into a cascade of little white bulges. He raised the binoculars to her face. He caught his breath. He felt his heart thud. He didn't blink: the woman was watching him. He held her gaze for a moment, then, discomfited, lowered the binoculars. When he looked up, the woman was writing again. Had he imagined it?

He drew the curtains and realised how hungry he was. He took a box of eggs from the fridge. As he beat them for an omelette, the memory of another woman came to his mind. He was at a friend's house. He must have been twelve or thirteen. They were playing football in the garden. A clumsy kick. The ball landed in a neighbour's garden. He stood waiting in the middle of the lawn while his friend went to fetch it. He looked over at the house. Behind the kitchen window, his friend's mother was leaning at the sink. She wore a sleeveless yellow dress. Her hair was tied back loosely. He thought she was beautiful. Her hands were wet, she used her wrist to push a lock of hair out of her eyes. He saw it in slow motion. At the same time she lifted her face towards him. Their eyes met. She smiled at him. The smile seeped slowly into him, condensed in his veins, weakened his muscles. His legs almost gave way. He turned away to hide the blush rising in his cheeks. That caress, that connection, he'd had a kind of intuition, but he'd never imagined... Not so strong, not so powerful. Even today he could still recall that smile, its searing tenderness, with perfect clarity.

She

How handsome you must be! Just as you were when
you were little. You still have, I am sure, the big,
curious, doe eyes that you fixed upon the world the
minute you were born. I imagine you tall, well-built
but not conscious of it, reserved but not shy, caring
with those you are close to. I picture you with a wide,
thoughtful face, a solemn mouth, Grecian nose, dark,
unkempt curls. I see you differently depending on
whatever random encounters I may have had that
day. A young man on the Metro or a group of students
walking gaily down the street are all it takes to make
me change my mind. Lately it has been more intense.
Perhaps because I have started writing to you. Your
presence is even more palpable. I am like a blind
person touching another's face. In this darkness I can
distinctly make out your features. Your disappearance
was not a disappearance, in the end, my only child
with a thousand human faces.

'What is essential is invisible to the eye,' as the
fox says to the Little Prince. How I would have loved
to read you that story, and so many others. When I
picture you, it is with my heart. And that is why, for
all the years of separation, I have to allow myself to
carry on conjuring up your image – but an image of
your heart, not of your eyes. A breach in the walls of
solitude and loneliness. My darling, my little boy, my
faraway son all grown up now.

He

He was sitting on an enormous bed hung around with heavy drapes. Tiny. All alone. A book lay open on his lap. He tried to read, but as he got to them the words vanished. In the distance, the indistinct sound of conversation. Who was talking? He yanked down a piece of fabric, but behind it was another, and another, and another. Who was talking? Answer me! At last he reached the final drape. Behind it: no one. The voices had fallen silent. Just the ocean, as far as the eye could see. Waves were lapping at the edge of the bed. The waters were rising. Or the bed was sinking. He was paralysed. He was terrified. Drops of his sweat mingled with the waves. He clutched the book to his chest. He tried to call for help. The words didn't emerge. Slowly he was immersed in the water until it was up to his neck. The bed had sunk. There was nothing to hold him up now. He was struggling to keep his head above the water. A huge wave was bearing down on him. He was about to drown.

He woke up.

He switched on the coffee percolator and stood watching it drip. The pile of dirty dishes had reached toppling point. In the time he took to deal with it the coffee was ready.

In the back of a cupboard, he unearthed a packet of biscuits. He poured himself some coffee and sat down at the table.

He began to draw his nightmare. The bed, the heavy drapes. The ocean. He drew himself on the bed, then changed his mind. He turned to a new page and started again. On the bed, the woman, lying down, the book alongside her. He quickly finished the sketch, then pushed it away to appraise it. It looked like the woman was dead. He drew a line through it. But that wasn't enough: he ripped out the page, crumpled it up and dropped it to the floor. Empty clichés. He tried again on a fresh page, and then another. Each attempt was like a skin shed and left behind. Or maybe simply an attempt to exorcise a bad dream. All of a sudden an image came back to him. It was in the street, through the café window. A movement. He grabbed the sketch-book he'd taken to the café. It was in there, he was sure of it. Somewhere among all the sketches he'd done that day. He flicked impatiently through the pages. A passer-by, from behind, walking away. He couldn't find it. He went back to the beginning and went through it again, more slowly. Eventually he found her, standing on the pavement. She was turning to wave goodbye. Just this gesture. Just right.

He propped a blank canvas up on the easel. It was wide as an empty stage. He took a deep breath, then picked up a piece of charcoal and sketched the street, the woman about to turn as she reached the corner. He focused on that: the way she turned, the hand bidding farewell. He was looking for the perfect inflection, the point where the gesture took on meaning. He adjusted the angle of the wrist, the curve of the fingers, until he found the delicate equilibrium, until he had grasped the captured, living image.

He went to find the other woman, the woman in the garden. He placed them side by side. In the garden, the woman's hand was raised to push aside a palm frond. But there was something else. She was protecting herself, perhaps, or hiding. Or shielding her eyes from a dazzling ray of sunlight. The new picture gave a different impression, even though it was just a sketch – this woman was not protecting herself. He thought it over. He wasn't sure. Still, it had something. The parting had already taken place, but an invisible thread still bound her to the person she was leaving behind. He hadn't drawn the other person. They weren't in the drawing, but you could see that they were still there in the way she nodded her head: We're saying goodbye, but I know you're still here. I'm taking a little part of you with me. That was what she was saying with this farewell. Everything was lodged in this detail, the clasp of the hand as she turned to leave. He picked up the charcoal and shaded in the wrist. The movement needed to be more supple. More delicate. It was a promise too, this hand clasping at nothing. It was saying something, as well as holding tight. Don't push them away. Hold on. That was better. Not quite there yet. But getting there.

He worked for several hours, without keeping track of time, in a great surge of momentum. It was as if he and the painting had become one. Everything else melted away. It was like surfing in Mauritius, the way he would catch the wave just as it broke. And then after a while, he had no idea how long it had been, when at last he reached the point where something he could never have explained, something he could only paint, appeared, when he'd got far enough that it could no longer escape, when his eyes began to blur, his arm had grown heavy, his stomach was aching with hunger – finally, he looked at his watch. Damn! It was gone eight already, he'd completely forgotten his dinner with Ariane. He ran his hand over his cheeks. Too late to shave. Never mind. He pulled on his jacket, rummaged in a drawer for a not-too-threadbare scarf, and hurried out.

He walked fast. Not so long ago he used to make this journey almost every day. On the way, he tried to focus his attention on this question: Ariane and he – where were they? They hadn't fought, they hadn't broken up. He was sure of that. And yet... something had changed, almost imperceptibly. Since when?

One morning, perhaps, not so long ago. He'd wanted to go home to paint, and she'd asked him to stay. He'd agreed. They spent a miserable afternoon together. He was preoccupied with his work. She tried to distract him. She wasn't herself. It was his fault. They'd ended up going to the cinema to see a terrible film. There was nothing she could do. Nor him.

Or it might have been the last time they'd seen each other, at an awful brunch with a group of her friends. It happens. Perhaps it was the noisy, stuffy, effortfully cool café. He paid no attention to the art world gossip and scandal. The shrieks of laughter. He went outside to smoke. She joined him. *Are you bored? Yes. Then go home.* The way she said it wasn't cold, it was more like an invitation. He left.

Their relationship no longer had the clarity there had been at the beginning. It was tarnished. He wasn't really himself with her anymore; Ariane was less spontaneous now too. He felt it. Daily life was getting in the way. Maybe that was all it was. Stupid daily life, like a cancer gnawing away at the things that really matter.

He walked into the restaurant and scanned the room. Ariane was sitting at a table towards the back with mirrors behind her. Her head was bowed. She wore an aquamarine sweater. He looked at her. His lover and a total stranger at the same time. He felt an intense, urgent desire for her. They were going to leave the restaurant right now, go to her place – no, to his – make love at once, surrounded by his paintings. A waiter asked him if he was waiting for someone. He shook his head and went over to join her. She half stood up but with the table between them their kiss was a little awkward. Their first sentences got tangled up. *I'm late. Don't worry, I was late too. I'm starving.* She disappeared behind the menu.

'What are you going to have?' He took her hand and squeezed it, hard.

'That hurts.' He let go. 'Sorry.'

He nodded to the waiter, watched as he and Ariane discussed various items on the menu. Her hair was knotted into a loose chignon that flattered her oval face. A few escaped tendrils rippled as she talked. She was beautiful. She was wearing black kohl around her eyes. When she smiled, tiny lines appeared at the corner of each one. He remembered the first time he'd noticed them. One morning he'd opened his eyes to find her looking at him. She didn't blink. Her look was tender. His flesh palpitated. The bedroom was warm. Like a hearth. He hadn't asked her anything, but her eyes held an answer. A fan of fine lines in the corner of each one when she smiled at him. That was the tipping point of their relationship. He only realised it now.

'Is the exhibition going ahead?'

So Marc had told her about it.

'Apparently.'

The crinkle of lines reappeared. He followed them, as though tracing them faintly with a dry nib. An 'I love you' rose to his lips but failed to emerge. The lines vanished.

'What are the paintings of?'

'Too early to say. Marc must have said, no?'

'Yes, he did.'

The waiter brought the wine. They stopped talking as he filled their glasses.

'He told me about a woman. He thought it seemed promising.'

'He said that?'

His question was lost in the hubbub. Ariane didn't reply, but he knew she wouldn't have made it up to please him. He had more faith in Ariane than in Marc. He looked at the fine gold chain she wore round her neck. Where the neck became the shoulder, just by a beauty spot, the links rose slightly over her collarbone. He thought of Titian. Not of a specific painting. Of Titian in general, the way he painted women's skin. Although maybe there was a particular painting. There must be a woman like that, a specific work, and one day he'd discover it for the first time with Ariane.

At the beginning of their relationship, they'd discussed art non-stop. It was all they talked about. It was almost crazy. A drug. They explored all the museums and galleries. She opened Paris up to him. They grew very close. She took him by the hand. He trusted her, more than he trusted anyone else, though they were forever disagreeing. Which was fine. Better even. Sometimes he managed to convince her, more often it was she who convinced him. She had more arguments up her sleeve, and was stubborn as a mule. 'What are you on about, you savage,' she'd say, laughing. Ultimately their opinions always converged. But it needed the two of them, together, to get to that point. He'd never experienced anything like it. Such happiness, coupled with trust. Something was growing between them.

Ariane seemed to be waiting for him to speak. She sipped her wine slowly, holding her glass between her hands. Something had changed. It was definitely because of him. Because of his art. He was withdrawing. He wasn't available anymore, or at any rate not as much. He ought to have been able to explain it to her: his anxiety about the exhibition, the woman who was hiding from view. It was just a phase. But there was a tension he couldn't shake. In fact he needed it, for himself, for his work.

'So what do you think?'

'Sorry?'

'Is it a good idea?'

She looked at him, confused.

'To paint a woman?' he said.

She smiled. Tendrils of hair danced merrily.

'How would I know? I haven't seen the paintings.'

'But you know my work. Imagine: I'm painting a woman. Not from life.' She raised an eyebrow. 'Not a specific woman. It could be any woman. A woman who appeared out of nowhere.' He recognised the glint in her eye. 'I know what you're going to say: she didn't really appear out of nowhere. Okay, let's say that's the case. But it's not the point.' He didn't let her speak. 'What I'm asking you is, is it a subject for an exhibition? I mean, is it a good subject?'

He stopped. He wanted to hear what she thought. She took his hand and turned it over, palm facing upwards. He didn't resist. She opened it and held it flat on the table, as if she were about to read his palm. She sighed.

'What a strange question... Obviously it's not a question of good or bad; it all depends how you approach it.' She folded his hand closed, as if she'd slipped something inside before returning it. He didn't move. 'Did you ask yourself that question about your earlier paintings?'

He shook his head.

'So why now?'

'I don't know. Age, maybe.'

It was a joke: he was far too young for that. Ariane ignored it. She seemed weary. She looked him straight in the eye.

'If you're not sure you have a good subject, maybe it's because your subject hasn't been born yet. You've intuited something, the material is there, it's somewhere inside you,' she pointed to her heart, 'you just haven't found its form yet.' She smiled. 'But you know all that already. You know it better than I do.'

She opened his hand again. She traced the curve of his fingers with her own. It was as if his hand, under hers, was no longer a part of him. It looked like a beetle lying on its back.

'Think about painting as a language, your language,

that's how you give meaning to things, the way you find your words. It's the painting that needs to be just right, not the subject. Be patient.'

He didn't answer. He had the feeling she hadn't said all she wanted to say. He picked up the bottle of wine and refilled her glass. She took it and raised it to her lips, then changed her mind and put it down without taking a sip.

'It's only by actually doing the work that your message will take shape, rendered in paint. Have faith. It's by doing it that you'll discover what it is you're looking for. Try to express what you see, to communicate it, to get as close as you can to what's true for you. Do you remember what Giacometti said? A sculpture isn't an object, it's an interrogation, a question, an answer. Of course, it's difficult because, essentially, there isn't one single answer, but there's yours. Your answers. And that's all that matters.'

She looked away from him. He thought of the sketches slumbering in the studio. Everything still felt very unclear. He was like a miner who had located a rich seam but was struggling to make a dent in the sheer wall of rock surrounding it. What he was searching for was behind it. He had no choice but to keep digging. It was the only way.

'If you're going to pull this off, your work has to take precedence over everything else.' She said this so softly he might almost have thought he had dreamed it. Was it a question or a statement? He couldn't tell. He nodded.

'Over everything else,' she repeated. 'Starting now. There's nothing more difficult, but nothing is definitive either – in art, or love.'

So this was where they were. The two of them. Their relationship. There was a price to pay. He didn't have a choice. She didn't either. She knew. She wouldn't have fallen in love with him if he'd been someone who wasn't prepared to take risks. This was what he understood. They had to get through it.

The conversation continued, but with this tangle in its wake. He asked her about herself, about her work. She told him about an artist she was writing about. He listened. He enjoyed her company. If he could have changed things, perhaps he would have done. The waiter cleared their plates. A silence lodged between them.

She half smiled, and said, 'At least I'll be able to write your catalogue.'

Was this an encouragement or a farewell? She'd often joked, 'Watch out, if we ever move in together, it will be a conflict of interest and I won't be able to write about your work.' He realised that if the exhibition were to go ahead, she would write the catalogue – but only if they split up. Once more she was asking nothing of him, except, basically, that he pursue his quest right to the end. Ariane understood his work better than anyone else.

He looked at her. She was concentratedly sweeping the crumbs on the tablecloth into a little pile. He saw, superimposed, a likeness of the woman in the apartment opposite, sitting at her desk, alone, beyond the void.

She

We played together that morning. It was our little
ritual. You would wake up and clamber onto my bed
like a little kitten, while your father got ready and
Paris was beginning to stir. The rest of the world
vanished, leaving us to enjoy a few minutes of cosy
bliss, just the two of us.

I must have woken early because I was reading
when you slipped into bed beside me. I can still
feel the softness of your infant skin. I can still smell
you, like a freshly baked brioche. I can still feel the
delight of your giggling, wriggling little body against
mine. Once you were comfortably snuggled up beside
me, you took the book from me and, with a deeply
serious air, began turning the pages. I kept tickling
and cuddling you, smothering you in kisses. You gave
me a stern look that meant: *Maman, let me read!*
You were imitating me. I laughed, feasted my eyes
on you, amazed; the quintessence of love. I took the
book from you, you pulled it back, I took it off you
again. *Mine! No, it belongs to Maman! No, it's mine!*
I tickled you more and you gurgled with laughter. The
postcard I was using as a bookmark slipped out onto
the floor. You jumped down like a little bird to pick it
up, then handed it to me with a proud look on your
face, and said, 'Belong to Maman.'

The postcard was a reproduction of the famous
Flemish painting, Jan van Eyck's Arnolfini portrait.

I'd bought it in London. The three of us had spent a weekend there together not long before. You climbed back into bed and we looked at the postcard together. I showed you the husband and wife. It bothered me slightly to be presenting you with such an austere portrait of a couple. I would have preferred a more cheerful image. I have always found the stark mystery of this portrait rather disturbing. Isn't it ironic that our life together should be bookmarked by this painting? I pointed out the little dog. There is something incongruous about the innocence of this fluffy little animal at the feet of the rigidly posed couple. I can still picture the adorable crease of concentration at the corner of your mouth. You ran your finger carefully over the image. You pointed at the man and said 'Papa'. I shuddered. You pointed to the woman and said, 'Maman'. I remember it like it was yesterday. Then it was time to get up. I tucked the postcard back inside the book, feeling a kind of weight in my stomach, not yet aware that the coming day was going to leave a deep wound in both our lives.

Yes, I remember it like it was yesterday. I've held onto the postcard all this time, though it is unbearably painful. It is proof that it was not all a dream.

He

It looked like she was writing more and more. He would watch her from his worktable or sitting in the armchair. When he was tired of painting, he'd turn towards the window and watch her. He began to draw her. She seemed to have changed. She was thinner, perhaps. He felt no sense of shame when he watched her. She was just an image within a room. She only existed in this frame, she wasn't real.

He sketched out the composition in broad strokes. The bed, the blanket, the velvet cushions. He opened a box of dry pastels. He played with the colours. Dark green and garnet. Then the books, the chest of drawers, the rug. Finally, the desk. He imagined what might be concealed behind the stretch of wall between the two windows. He liked the way she momentarily disappeared when she walked across the room. There she was, there she wasn't, there she was again. It gave him a little frisson, like he was a small boy playing a game of peekaboo: 'Where's she gone?' then she was back, 'Ah, here she is!' She existed only within the diptych of these two windows, both familiar and unknown. He never wondered what she did when she left the room, or after she drew the curtains. She vanished; she didn't exist anymore.

He grew acquainted with her schedule. Around seven, knowing she would be home soon, he'd glance up mechanically, even before she turned on the light.

Sometimes, in the morning, when he stood at the window smoking his first cigarette, she'd already have left, the curtains were open, the room empty. Weekends didn't change things very much. She didn't sleep in. He never saw a visitor. She was always on her own in the bedroom. He never saw her naked. She always closed the curtains before she got undressed. Once or twice only he saw her changing the sheets in the morning. She pulled off the sheets, rearranged the green and garnet cushions. She put her clothes away in the chest of drawers and stacked her books on the shelves or piled them on the floor.

From the chest of drawers to the bed. From the bed to the desk. The same trajectories, repeated. Came in, went out. Straight to the desk. The same movements. Opening or closing a book. Head down. Head in hand. Reading. Writing. Hair up or loose. Sometimes she spoke on the phone. She'd stop, mid-movement, freeze – struck by an idea, perhaps, or trying to hold onto a thought or to grasp something impalpable.

If only she'd turn towards him again. Just once. Yet he never turned on the light. He sat there in the gloom. Watching her.

She

That afternoon, after work, I went to pick you up from nursery. My heart soared as always at the prospect of sweeping you into my arms and giving you a big hug. I practically ran, filled with the thought of seeing you. Every evening it was the same arc of eager anticipation followed by pure joy.

When I arrived, as always my eyes scanned the lively group of children to find you. I marvelled at the sight of each child immersed in an activity: having tea in the Wendy house, playing with building blocks, riding a tricycle, each child completely absorbed, committed, uninhibited. If I didn't see you right away, I would get a twinge in my solar plexus, a hint of anxiety that I knew would only make the thrill of seeing you more intense. Often, once I had spotted you, and if you hadn't seen me first, I would stop myself from running over and picking you up so I could savour the pleasure of watching you. I remember one time, you were sitting at the little red table, drawing with such concentration that you didn't notice me come in. Still today, this image is more vivid than if I was looking at a photograph. Your brown curls and pursed lips, your chubby little hand gripping the felt tip pen. I kept a lot of your drawings. I often take them out to look at them. Maybe it's a mother's vanity, but I have always thought they were rather wonderful.

So anyway, that evening I got to the nursery. I looked around for you. I didn't even have time to panic. One of the assistants came up to me looking surprised. Your father had already come to get you. I thought there must have been a misunderstanding. I said it was impossible, he was still at work. She told me he had come by in the morning to pick you up for your paediatrician appointment. I was confused. You didn't have an appointment.

I rushed out of the nursery and ran to our apartment. I raced up the stairs four at a time, tipped the contents of my handbag out on the landing to find my keys. My hands were shaking as I fumbled for the lock, and when the door opened, after the dash up the stairs that I still relive endlessly in my nightmares, after minutes had passed that seemed like an eternity, as soon as I looked around the apartment, I knew something had changed. I didn't even try to rationalise. I didn't try to quell my overwhelming panic. Every step I took in the apartment, every empty drawer, every wardrobe whose door swung open, confirmed what I could not bear to comprehend: your father had packed up and left, taking you with him.

I would have liked to persuade myself, at that moment, that he had only taken you away temporarily. But alone there in our gutted home, an instinctive conviction screamed at me that it was much more serious than that. All the clues from the previous days and months suddenly came together like the pieces of a puzzle. That was what I told the police. That was the guilt that haunted me: I hadn't predicted it, I hadn't guessed how far he would go. He hated me. He wanted to make me suffer as much as he could. The police interrogated us – me, our friends, his mother, his colleagues. They examined bank statements, looked for train and plane reservations. All this wasted time went by, confirming the obvious: your father had decided to rip you away from me to punish me.

Yes, 'rip you away' is the right expression. I was amazed that I could still breathe. I was baffled that my heart was still beating.

I would have given everything. I did give everything I could: my days, my nights, every spark of my energy, every second of my life. I was consumed by my desperation to find you. Even after the police had called off the search, I continued looking. I placed ads in local newspapers. I posted flyers with photographs of you and your father in mailboxes and stuck missing person posters up in shops. I hired private investigators. I never gave up. People thought I was crazy, and perhaps I was. But not looking would have made me even crazier. I was sick with despair, with disbelief, with rage: against your father and against the whole world and its impotence in the face of your disappearance. To know you were alive, somewhere, but not to know where, not to be able to see you grow up, not to be able to hold you, was the cruellest torture imaginable.

I saw no other way out than to keep on searching for you. I could not die because of you; I could not live without you.

He

He hurried through the entrance of the Metro station like Pinocchio into the belly of the whale. It was at least a couple of months since he'd last been to visit the old lady. He didn't miss her or anything, but he couldn't stop seeing her entirely. Or maybe he could. In any case, he'd told her he was coming today. At the end of the corridor, he saw a train drawing into the platform; he quickened his pace, made it through the doors just as they were closing. He slid into a seat. He pictured the old lady sitting in her armchair, back ramrod straight. Almost as dusty as the antiques in her drawing room. She had known his father. They could talk about certain things. He sniggered to himself. He might as well talk to a wall.

He looked around at the other passengers. It was the same as in the café: mentally he'd trace a neck, a mouth, a wrinkle, the angle of a wrist. He was beginning to regret having told the old lady he would pay her a visit. He should have been working. He could already picture her expression: the way she had of looking him up and down when he arrived. Inspected and judged. The feeling of being denounced. The same look his father used to mete out every morning before he left for school. Not a word. Just that look. The terrible judgement. The nebulous sense of guilt for not having done what he was supposed to have done. Without ever knowing what that was.

In his head he still thought of her as the Old Lady, because one Christmas when he was a child she had sent him a copy of *Babar*. This was before he'd met her, and he imagined that this friend of his father's, who was old enough to be his grandmother, who lived in France, in the great city of Paris, and who had been described to him as a distinguished woman, must be just like the old lady in the book. Her name was Geneviève. That was what he had been told, but he'd understood it as *jeune vieille,* "old young". And indeed, when he did eventually meet her for the first time, his first thought was that even when she was young, she must have looked old. Or maybe she had never been young. Like a witch. She was hundreds of years old. Nothing like the lady in *Babar*.

She was the only person who ever came to see them in Mauritius. The only link they still had with France, even though that was where he was born. He had lived in Paris until he was three years old. That was what he'd been told. Of course, he had no recollection of it. Jeune Vieille had known his father's parents, his grandparents. He had never met them: they died before he was born. In a way she was their only family. 'I am a little like your grandmother,' she said to him sometimes when his father wasn't there, as if it were a secret between them. If he had to have a grandmother, he would not have chosen her.

In the last few years of his father's life he'd pretty much forgotten about Jeune Vieille. From time to time his father spoke of her to him, but he never saw her anymore. She was too frail to make the journey to Mauritius. He didn't want to go and see her in France. Sometimes his father went without him. When his father died, he contacted her to tell her the news. Despite her age, she'd insisted on making the trip. The morning of the funeral, he walked by the terrace outside his father's office and saw her sitting at the window, weeping. He couldn't hear her, but he watched her, head in hands, shoulders shaking. It wasn't so much the intensity of her grief that struck him, but rather the impression that there was a huge, crushing weight on her shoulders. At the cemetery, however, she stood upright and impassive, as was her wont. He invited her to say a few words, but she declined.

She stayed for several days and helped him sort through his father's personal effects: clothes and documents. He let her do it. It was a relief. There was nothing he wanted to keep. Essentially, the reason he visited her now that he was living in Paris was to thank her for having dealt with all that stuff.

The Metro drew into a station and braked. People got off. A memory came back to him. He was looking at puppets behind glass. It was terribly cold. His father had taken him to a department store to buy him a warm coat. He was young, no more than eight or ten. It was Christmas. His first time in Paris. Jeune Vieille was unwell, so, exceptionally, he and his father had come to France. It was the first time they had left Mauritius together. What an adventure! He was disappointed there was no snow. The city wasn't white, it was grey. Nonetheless, there were things he liked: the noises, the shapes, the light that was so different. The ladies were elegant. His mother must have looked like them. She and his father had met in Paris. One day he was going to live there.

In the windows of the department store, Christmas elves were wrapping up toys by the thousands, just as in the song playing through the loudspeakers. He tugged his father's hand to make him slow down. He wanted to watch. Gifts were being wrapped and rewrapped, over and over again; the sleigh was gliding in a loop; Santa Claus disappeared down the chimney and then popped back up again. So many automatons, getting ready for Christmas, wrapping, straightening up, waving, wrapping, straightening up, waving. The scene slowly turned. Huge flakes of snow fell interminably behind the glass. The actions were endlessly repeated. The elves smiled into the void. Santa's moustache was coming unstuck on one side. His father's arm was pulling him along, but he resisted. He tried to free himself, but the hand tightened. A chill ran up his arm. He had to free his hand. He had to get away, or they would put him in the window, with the horrible elves and the fake Santa.

The train braked again. Something caught his eye. Hair tied back with a clip. A few feet away from him, the woman, sitting with her back to him, leaning forward slightly. Was it possible? She looked older. He could only see a sliver of her profile. The resemblance was striking but the context so different. His heart thudded in his chest. He thought to himself, *there's nothing surprising about this, it's totally normal that she should be on the Metro.* She'd got up from her desk, put on her coat, picked up her handbag. She'd gone down the staircase and stepped out of the building into the street. Her heels had tip-tapped along the pavement, one after the other, until she reached the entrance to the Metro, the same one he'd walked through shortly after. The bedroom, the

Metro. The two images collided. The woman was real. He could have stood up and moved to the other end of the carriage to get a better look. He didn't. It was she who stood up. She came towards him. He was transfixed. She was standing just inches from him. He felt her warmth. He heard her breath. It was now or never. He raised his eyes. She looked at him. A fleeting moment. The train stopped and the doors opened. She turned away and got off. The doors closed. He didn't react. The train began moving again. He was still sitting down. He hadn't moved at all. On the platform, the woman walked away.

It all happened so quickly. She had been about to tell him something. He was sure of it. That expression in the painting. The eyes he couldn't capture. There, inches away from him, the woman whispered something to him. She hadn't spoken; she made no movement. It was all in her expression. Those eyes, that woman. A great wave of exhaustion broke over him. He'd just missed his station.

She

Let me pause here.

You are so alive.

Is it right for me to be stirring up all these old memories?

Grief is so easily reawakened.

I really ought to stop this letter.

What is the point of it?

Is it just the project of an unhinged old woman without much time left? I am sure that's what you'll think if it ever reaches you. Yes, I do feel awfully old. Waiting doesn't halt time. It doesn't make it pass more slowly either. That's an illusion. Sometimes, while I'm waiting for the group of visitors that I am going to guide through the labyrinth of the museum, I find myself staring at the clock face and it makes me feel dizzy. How can it be that when my life stopped the clock's hand continued to turn? How can any of this be real? How is it possible that time keeps ticking away? Surely this is a parenthesis, a dream from which I am going to wake up. I'll see you before me and life will start over again.

My little one, I love you and I will keep searching for you until my dying breath.

He

He saw the way she looked at his sweater and jeans as he walked into the living room.

'Well, well, well! In my day, a tramp would have been better dressed. Come, sit down and pour me some tea.'

She chattered away as he did what he was told. His mind was still on the woman in the train. He almost couldn't believe that their paths had just crossed.

'Are you listening to me?'

The old lady was thin, her voice light and reedy. Even in the clammy heat of Mauritius, she was always impeccably turned out. Her pale pink silk blouse floated over her gaunt body. Her hair was perfectly set. He had never seen her with so much as a hair out of place. There was a sour smell of face powder and hairspray mingled with dust.

'Have you lost weight, Geneviève?'

'Yes. I have no appetite now. One loses interest in everything at my age. Except in dying with dignity.' She turned her head towards the kitchen. 'You'll help me, won't you, Samira? You'll help me die with dignity?' She raised her voice so her carer could hear. Without waiting for the 'Yes, yes, madam', she went on, 'I'm falling apart; bones, cartilage, organs, my head soon, no doubt; and to top it all, I'm losing my memory. I make a fool of myself at bridge. I shan't be around for much longer, believe you me. The Lord will summon me soon.' There was no answer to that. He took a sip of tea. He didn't like it. 'But you have your whole life ahead of you.'

She stopped talking to drink her tea. Her heavy rings slid around her scrawny fingers. She presided like an aged regent. Preserved in formalin, like something straight out of the Musée Grévin, she sat straight in her armchair, with her hands on the armrests. He was reminded of Bacon's portrait of Pope Innocent X. He imagined her pulverised by his brushstrokes, enormous, dripping splatters. Rain beat against the windows.

'Look at this weather. Samira, did you close the window in my bedroom? We shan't be going out in this. And as for the cold... It's not like Mauritius! One has to wonder why you came to live here.' The endless litany. 'You were very happy there.'

The same tone of voice as his father, when he'd snap at him, 'Stop getting under my feet.' He said it all the time.

'Remind me why you are in France?'

'For my painting, Geneviève.'

'Your painting? Ah yes, the pictures. But still, you would be far better off in Mauritius. All things considered, you had a very nice life there.'

He put down his cup carelessly. A few translucent, coppery drops of tea slopped onto the tray.

'But why Mauritius, Geneviève?'

She looked at him blankly.

'What made my father leave Paris for Mauritius?'

She set down her teacup. One of her rings knocked against the porcelain with a dull chink.

'You know perfectly well why – for work. You do know that, don't you? For his work.'

'Well, there you go, it's the same thing. I came to Paris for my work.'

'What work?'

'My painting, Geneviève.'

'Oh yes! Is it going well?'

She never asked to see his paintings. She hadn't come to his first exhibition.

'Yes and no. My gallerist has offered me another exhibition in September.'

'September is a long way away.'

'It doesn't seem that far off, actually.'

'Obviously, when you have your whole life ahead of you – incidentally, I wanted to tell you...' She paused.

'Yes?'

Her fingers reached for the crucifix on the small table beside her.

'Since your father's death, I have felt so much closer to Him, our Lord. In my pain, you know, I glimpse the Virgin's pain. She helps me. Yes, you need to know this: she brings me a great deal of succour.'

Another one of her sanctimonious outbursts. He stifled a sigh. When she used to visit them in Mauritius, he often had to go with her to church. It bored him to death. The worst was when she'd come to his room at bedtime and make him say his prayers. He did it mechanically, impatient for her to go back to the living room and sit with his father.

'He alone is the judge, but I see Mary's sufferings as the paradigm of divine motherly love. The death of the Son, you understand, and the cross he had to bear... for a mother to experience that... the trials that her son endured...'

He was only half listening. His gaze wandered to the wall behind her, where a portrait of an old general sporting a medal hung. Her husband. From the upper part of the frame, the general frostily observed the scene. Even as a child, he had been struck by this portrait. The man had died a long time ago. He'd never known him, but he reminded him of his father. It could have been something about the hairline, or the cleft in his chin, or the stiffness of the pose. His austere bearing. Like the old lady. A question of 'milieu'? She was always going on about that. 'Our milieu', 'from the same milieu', 'in such a milieu'. It was like a ceremonial sword that dubs or ostracises. She was, her father was, the general was, they all were from the same 'milieu'. The right one, it went without saying. It was a notion that made absolutely no sense to him. Especially having grown up in Mauritius. And still today. What is a milieu? Like an environment? The marine environment, the mountainous environment, cold environments... He didn't feel like he belonged to any environment, any milieu. Looking at the general's portrait made him think more than anything of manacles and blinkers. A perch for birds of ill omen.

'Geneviève, you know when you went through my father's papers? Did you really not find a single photograph of my mother?'

She took a sharp intake of breath.

'You have asked me this many times. And I've told you already, no, I did not find any. Photographs and souvenirs were not your father's thing. You know what he was like. He didn't have time for emotion.'

Something about the tone of this sentence... different,

somehow. Geneviève never used to criticise his father. But since his death there had been a shift in the way she spoke about him. Almost negligible, but there. Grafted onto her unconditional approval was just the hint of a reproach.

She resumed her sanctimonious homily. He didn't listen. His gaze turned to the convex mirror that hung on the wall. The reflection of the room, distorted. It had always intrigued him. The stretched, curved lines, the exaggerated perspective. And that bizarre hollow of light: the reflection of the window, the heavy curtains. It looked like an eye, with eyelids. The eye of a cyclops, in which the old lady was tiny, reduced to an insignificant detail, a wriggling maggot. The question resurfaced: did she really know nothing about his mother?

The little bug in the mirror squirmed slightly. 'Nothing at all. Nothing more than you've already been told.'

'Did my father really never talk to you about her?'

'You know he didn't like to talk about her. All that is ancient history. Like me. You must stop bothering me about it. There is no point in digging up the past.'

She began to wheeze. She gave a little cough. His father had said more or less the same thing: it's not right to rifle through other people's things.

He had been invited over to play at a friend's house. His father didn't dare object this time: the friend was the son of his boss. The house had huge windows that looked out onto the sea. He thought it was magnificent: the living room furnished with sunlight, like on a boat. He had stood in there for a while on his own. Timidly, he looked around. On the furniture and the walls, people were smiling. Photographs. In frames of all different shapes and sizes. His friend, his friend's parents, other people. Family members or friends. On boats, in gardens, in front of monuments, landscapes, Christmas trees and birthday cakes. They were very beautiful.

When he got home, he went into his father's study and began searching. At home there were no photographs. He opened drawers, files, folders. He lifted cushions, looked under the furniture, climbed on chairs, opened boxes. He took the books out of the bookcase, one by one, and shook their pages. Eventually he found one. A small, yellowing rectangle of glossy card escaped from a technical encyclopaedia, like victory falling on exhausted troops. He picked it up: his father and a young woman, posing before the entrance to a church, holding hands. He looked at the woman for a long time. She was beautiful. She was smiling. This was his mother.

He put the encyclopaedia away and took the photograph. He hid it under his bed. Every evening, after his father had been to check he was in bed, after he'd closed the door and the sound of his footsteps had faded away, he would sit up and study her. He would stare at his mother's face for as long as he could without blinking, until his eyes stung. They would fill with tears and blur his vision, and it seemed to him then that beneath the glossy patina the woman was alive.

One evening, the photograph wasn't under the bed. He checked ten times. Perhaps he had forgotten to put it away. He searched in his sheets, in every corner of the room. He had to face it then. He stood there, numb, then vomited his rage into his pillow in stifled punches, biting his lips to keep from screaming. The next day, as he was leaving for school, his father spoke to him from the kitchen. 'It's not nice to rifle through other people's things. I suggest you ponder this while you're at school today.'

So he learned not to think about it. What he had been told all these years could be summed up in three sentences: You were three years old; she drowned; her body was never found.'

'Samira, you may clear the tea things away.' This was the signal for him to leave. 'I won't see you out. You know the way.'

As he walked out of the front door, she muttered something else. He couldn't quite make out what she said, except, perhaps, these three words, 'Go in peace.'

She

I have not returned to this letter for several days. Reliving this nightmare has been hard. But now I have come back to it; I feel up to it again. However painful it is, I think one must never be afraid to face the truth. Secrecy is a festering wound; the truth may be harrowing but it's healthy.

Since I opted for this letter, I have to see it through. As much for myself as for you. I can't leave behind a zone of darkness. You wouldn't forgive me. So, why did your father want to punish me? I'm going to tell you, with the candour that only the passage of time allows. You're an adult now. If ever you read these lines, you'll want to know. If you grew up with your father, as I imagine you did, I won't have to tell you much for you to understand the rest. But first you have to accept one thing: this isn't the time for grievances and accusations, bitter fruits that rot the heart and warp the mind. Don't let it change the way you think about him, don't condemn him out of hand. I know he loved you, in his own way. That certainty was a glimmer of light, however faint, in the darkness of your loss. The person he wanted to suffer was me, I am quite sure of that. The fact that you grew up far away from your mother must have seemed to him simply unavoidable collateral damage. Maybe he even convinced himself that it was better for you that way. I want to believe that he tried to make up for my absence with extra helpings of love. Perhaps he remarried, maybe you grew up with someone else, maybe she is more your mother than I. It's a possibility I have thought about, hated, and wished for all at the same time.

I began making plans to leave your father shortly after you were born. Since the wedding, his behaviour towards me had gradually changed. Your birth, and my love for you, only accelerated the inexorable deterioration. At first, I attributed his insistence that I sever my relationships with the rest of the world to the joy of your birth. I saw my friends less and less. Even my conversations with colleagues at the pharmacy were reduced to a minimum. I did stand my ground about one thing: against his wishes, I went back to work at the end of my maternity leave. This earned me endless recriminations and criticism; I was a bad mother because I refused to stay at home to take care of you, because I chose to work, to the detriment of my child. He never missed an opportunity to point this out. Whenever you were ill, he blamed me. Every so often, for no particular reason, he would decide to pick you up from nursery. He would bring you home and rain down abuse on me because when he got there your nappy was soiled, or your clothes were dirty, a thousand shortcomings for which he held me responsible. I found you a place in a different nursery, thinking that would placate him, but he didn't like the new crèche any more than the old one, and now he held it against me that you had to wake up earlier because it took longer to get there. I didn't know what to do to be worthy of his love. I didn't feel

I was worthy of anything anymore. Nothing I did was good enough for him, and I was bewildered by his demands. I felt like I was trapped in a maze. And yet whenever we bumped into friends or acquaintances, he would sing my praises, extol my dedication and show you off with pride. He'd say, with a laugh, that everything good about his son could only have come from me. My hopes would be raised again, and I'd remember when we first met, the sheer happiness of those early days, our mutual admiration and love. But the lull was always short-lived.

A kind of survival instinct told me that something strange was going on. Your father did all he could to convince me that I was the problem. Later I went to see psychologists, not so much to confirm my suspicions, but out of fear that he might one day turn this violence against you. I think my mind was put to rest. I hope with good cause. Only you would be able to tell me.

No matter how much he towed me towards darkness, you always led me back to the light. You were my infinite reserve of love and happiness, my inexhaustible strength. With you I experienced for the first time what love really is. When you came into the world, those first moments when your body was placed onto mine, the reality of you, your eyes lifted towards me, your vulnerability, were like a detonator. The walls I was suffocating inside were blown apart. Suddenly I was alert, I was alive, I loved and I was loved. I learnt what that really meant. Do you have even the slightest idea of what you showed me? Motherhood is a doorway that opens onto infinity.

Your tiny feet and fingers, the fold of your neck, the curve of your tummy, your perfect lips, your eager eyes; what an endless miracle it all was. And now I was conscious of the prison your father wanted to keep me locked up inside. I hammered at its walls. And the more I hammered at them, the more I tried to break them down, the more he reinforced them. It reminds me of Sylvia Plath: 'To the one who lies under the bell jar, blank and stopped and frozen like a dead baby, the world itself is a bad dream.' You woke me up. It's no coincidence that that was the moment I allowed another man – a man who was not your father – to get close to me. I was hypersensitive. My senses were exquisitely receptive. Your existence elated me. Forgive me.

I blame myself for not having guessed that your father would destroy me if I tried to escape. He rejected the idea of divorce out of hand. The mere mention of it unleashed in him an uncontrollable fury. I could have put up with any number of blows except the one he eventually selected to strike me with. How did I not realise that you would be the weapon he would choose? If I had realised, believe me I would never have brought up the idea of leaving. I would never have mentioned it to him. I would have found another way. I would never, ever have deprived you of your mother. I didn't want to lose you. I have no idea what your father told you about me. I have tried to imagine every possible scenario. What did he tell you about me for all those years? Did he make you hate me, or did he just pretend I never existed? Whatever the case, now you know the truth of what happened, if only some brief details. I am still your mother, and what I want more than anything is the assurance that you did not suffer. I want to know that you grew up supported and loved.

When a tree is thrashed by the wind, it grows bowed. When it is exposed to drought, it produces fewer leaves. People are the same, they adapt. But beware of the cracks beneath the surface. Don't respond to drought with parsimoniousness; don't choose anger to stave off a gale; don't let silence take root in solitude. Don't retreat into yourself.

He

He went home on foot. He needed to breathe after his visit to the old lady. The clouds were low in the sky. The light was flat. He strode. He inhabited his body as though it were a garment that was too big for him. Should he go to a café? There were none nearby. Just walls of stone as far as the eye could see. He lit a cigarette. Jeune Vieille's words were still tangled up in his head. If he carried on walking, they would eventually fade away. He walked past people standing mechanically to attention under a canopy of trees.

He pictured his father's terrace. All his plants, neatly arranged in pots. The daily inspection. Impeccable rows. He even trained the unruly bougainvilleas with cordons until they looked like barbed wire. If a semblance of growth, something spontaneous, appeared, he pruned it or dug it up. Halt, dandelion, who goes there! He scarified the compacted soil. The roots had to breathe. He did it all first thing in the morning, every single day, until his last day on earth. That morning, the bougainvilleas, the lantanas and the others had their revenge: his father collapsed with no warning at their feet. Under their indifferent gaze. There were never any bougainvilleas in his paintings.

There was another postcard from Ariane in the mailbox. He waited until he got upstairs to read it. He settled into the armchair. It was a portrait of Giacometti by Cartier-Bresson. The artist was moving one of his sculptures across his studio. He was in motion, like the sculpture, but unlike the sculpture he was slightly out of focus. On the back she had written:

And you, great soul, do you expect to dream
of lying colours that no longer seem
like waves or gold made here for fleshy eyes?

He smiled. He passed his hand over his cheek. He traced his jawline with his fingers, the way Ariane did. Maybe he should call her. See her. Drop by her house. He looked at the postcard again: the artist, blurred, in movement. Material in the making. He stood up. He looked around for a catalogue. He knew the one. He was sure he'd seen it recently, on the floor, in a pile of books. He shoved the books with his hands, with his feet, as if he were a bit drunk. Eventually he found it. It was Ariane who had given it to him: an old catalogue from a Cartier-Bresson exhibition. He found the photograph of Giacometti, and two others. He studied it closely. The artist. His sculptures. He wanted to understand what it was that Cartier-Bresson had captured. The sculptor was blurred, the sculptures in focus. His own confusion was clarified, momentarily, in the sculptures. Not in him. His quest had no respite and no end. The object that has been created is free, has found its form. But then immediately the urge to go further forces him to carry on.

Yes, sometimes there was a ray of light, an equilibrium, an opening, at the point where his effort culminated, where his vision took shape. Then he had to start again, because deep down there was still this

swirling confusion. The form appeared, then frag-
mented. Would another be born in its place, generated
by the previous one? From one birth to another, one
failure to the next. The questioning never stopped. The
artist is always confused. The soul of Giacometti, of the
artist, was in this blurred figure. Ariane was right, he
had to keep trying to find what it was he was looking
for.

She

I reread my last words: *Don't retreat into yourself.* I
am aware of the irony of such counsel. I'm not sure
I managed it myself. Your father had an excellent
aim: I wanted to reclaim my freedom, he found the
way to keep me locked up. Yes, I admit it, after your
kidnapping the bell jar closed over me again. Once
more I was living in a nightmare.

Nothing and nobody could help me. The man I
was with certainly tried. He did everything he could,
but I was dead inside. I let him into my life for a
while. Then I booted him out because he stopped me
thinking about you. I needed a designated culprit, and
there he was, ready-made. He gave me love; I held
him responsible. He offered me support; I turned him
away. What I wanted was to wake up with you, every
morning. I needed for you still to be there. All I had
left was your memory to cherish. Very well then, in
that case I decided I would never let it go. It was more
than that even; holding onto you inside me was to
pledge that the day I found you, things would go back
perfectly naturally to the way they had been before.
Carrying on living with you was the guarantee that
one day it would happen.

Don't worry, I wasn't doing it for you. I didn't
sacrifice myself. I wasn't punishing myself, wallowing
in my misfortune. Not at all. A mother would
understand this. Perhaps you're already a father.

Maybe you understand. You never stopped being the source of all my happiness, my little one, my darling boy. Even though you weren't there, you still accompanied me wherever I went. I knew you were alive somewhere. Did you think I was dead? I have no idea what your father told you. But I knew you were alive. Our closeness, our connection, our communication had to endure. So that the day we found each other I would be ready. So that nothing, not a single day, would be lost.

That's why I bade this man farewell. I didn't have the strength to give you up for him. I repeat: don't think you stopped me from living. I was still alive; I was still a mother; that was all I wanted. You were always there, inside me. As time passed you were buried more deeply, but the space you occupied didn't shrink. Like a pregnant woman, I was filled with joy to be carrying you inside me. My darling boy.

This way of seeing things probably seems quite mad to you, or even tragic. You're wrong though. I found a new equilibrium, a way to stay alive. Instead of choosing death, I chose life. In spite of the bell jar, I found a way to keep from suffocating.

Let me try to explain by recounting a memory from that time. It might not seem significant to you, but sometimes something apparently trivial can act as an unexpected, restorative wake-up call. This incident was a turning point.

I had stuck up missing person posters on the trees all along our street. One day I went out and the first thing I noticed was that the posters were gone. I felt like I'd been punched in the stomach.

It was as if you'd been snatched from me a second time. I refused to accept your erasure. My entire life was reduced to my sorrow and my search for you, and now they were being negated. At the end of the road I saw the person responsible, a streetsweeper taking down the last few posters. I rushed towards him like a fury. I swore at him. I reached into his cart to retrieve the posters. He stood there, bewildered. I unleashed on him all the hatred and bitterness I had been suppressing. Then I went home to find a roll of tape, with the firm intention of going out and sticking the posters back up. When I came outside I found myself face to face with the streetsweeper. He was waiting for me. He spoke first, probably for fear that I was about to start hurling insults at him again.

That moment is engraved on my memory with astonishing clarity. I remember his face perfectly, the way his hands gripped the broom, the way he kept his eyes fixed on the ground. 'Madame, everyone in the neighbourhood knows what happened to you. We are all very sorry. It's so horrible, what happened to you. I understand, believe me. But it's been almost a year now. Don't you think that if anyone had seen your husband' – he lowered his voice as he articulated the word – 'or your child, they would have said something? Don't you agree that these posters don't do anything now except make people sad, you more than anyone else? They're the first thing people see in the morning when they leave the house. Madame, it's not your fault! You have done everything you could. But the posters can't help now. Your son, he must be somewhere with his father. He's living his life. Maybe you need to start living yours now too.'

As he spoke, this man I didn't know raised his head and looked me in the eye. He had the gentlest, kindest expression I had ever seen. I went back inside and burst into tears. I hadn't cried in months. The man, the way he looked at me, made my anger melt away.

And so I began to find my feet again. The man's words became my lifeline. 'He is living his life. Maybe you need to start living yours now too.' So, slowly but surely, rage became hope and I made my way back to the shore. I seized that glimmer of hope and draped it over my days. Perhaps I will even see you again.

He

He set to work. He had an idea for a new piece. The feel of the charcoal comforted him like a friendly handshake. The woman, sitting in a glassed-in veranda. On a pedestal table next to her was a songbird in a cage. She was resting her head on one arm outstretched on the table alongside the cage. She looked as though she was asleep, but her eyes were open. The plants were growing around her like a virgin forest. Through the foliage could be seen flashes of the metal structure of the veranda. The windows were darkened by the night. It was pitch black outside. The light came from inside, casting an intense chiaroscuro through the plants. The woman's legs were in shadow. There was an undulating form at her feet that looked at first glance like a liana – there were lots of them. Or perhaps a bar of the chair or the foot of a table. But the form was alive. Now it was clear what it was, with its sinuous body and the bulge of the head. A snake. Yet the woman sat there, impervious. Surely someone should warn her, make her realise the urgency, but she remained composed and unruffled, listening to the trill of the songbird.

Ariane's words came back to him: with hard work, whatever you want to say will take shape. And there he was, in front of the impenetrable wall, hacking away at it with all his strength. He needed time. He knew he'd made the right choice, and that she understood him. He worked without stopping. Barely sleeping or eating. Hours slipped by, dispatching the day then resurrecting it. Swipe after swipe. Brushstroke after brushstroke. He saw only her. He captured the way she moved. He followed the shape of her body. He stroked her skin. He held her hands. He untied her hair, inclined her head, put a blush in her cheek, traced the line of her nose, kissed her mouth, inhaled her breath. He held his paintbrush still in mid-air: mingled with the scent of the flowers, he caught a hint of her perfume.

When he finished, he went over to the bookshelf. He browsed the spines for a few moments, then pulled out the poetry book he was looking for. It was growing dark. He sat down in the armchair. Rather than turn on the light, he placed a candle on the windowsill. It was something he liked to do, it reminded him of when he was little, lighting candles in church and praying for the impossible.

Nightfall raised the curtain on the apartments across the courtyard. The old lady on the first floor was doing the dishes leaning against the sink like it was a prie-dieu. The young couple were silhouetted against the flickering light of the television. The child's room was ready for bedtime. The flux of lives, separate and indifferent to one another. His gaze lingered on the dark windows of the woman's apartment. He opened the book of poems. The floating halo of the candle made the lines dance. 'First paint a cage... long years... deepest silence... if the bird doesn't sing...' He let the book fall into his lap. The candle flame flickered. The easel's shadow quivered. From the depths of the darkness rose a forgotten voice: 'Sing, sweet nightingale...' He staggered over to the bed and collapsed. On his cheek, the faintest graze of a kiss.

She

I've come to Naples for a few days. I've escaped, on
a whim. Death might be staring me in the face, but
it doesn't scare me. I've come to meet it at the place
where Virgil and the Ancients located the door to the
Underworld. I feel like I am brazenly consorting with
death here. This is a country where the earth might
quake at any moment, where lovers embrace while
caressing the bronze skulls of souls in Purgatory.

My favourite time is early morning. I go down and
sit on the terrace of the café next door. The pavement
is too narrow, so two small plastic tables have been
set by the side of the street, wedged up by the parked
cars. A few feet away a street hawker sells cigarettes.
Local men come in to prop up the bar, buttonholing
each other at the door and holding forth before they
get going with their day. Women hurry past, towing
recalcitrant children by the arm on the way to school.
Drivers sound their horns for the least reason. I never
feel more alive than when I'm in the middle of all this
mayhem.

Yesterday I went to see the famous veiled Christ,
laid out in the middle of the chapel. He's made of
marble, but it's almost as if you can see him breathing.
I stood contemplating him for a long while. Tourists
came and went. I couldn't take my eyes off the outline
of the young man's body beneath the veil. He has such

a strong presence that when you look at him it's like you're touching him. I could feel the tension in his muscles, the swoop of his bones, almost the warmth of a living body. His head tilts a little to one side, as if weighted by deep sleep, in a pose that is completely uncontrived and peaceful. The serene expression on his face is profoundly moving. No fear or pain in this evocation of eternal repose, but an infinite quietude that moved me to tears.

Now I'm writing to you from my table outside the café. Some shouting has just broken out and interrupted my train of thought. Not an argument, just a couple of people greeting each other with ebullience. I love the ebb and flow of Neapolitan street life. I long for its insolence and its insouciance, like a fast-flowing river. The barista recognises me now. The way he speaks warms me like the sun. I only understand one word in three; he mixes Italian and Neapolitan dialect. He tells me about his city. He loves it, madly, like a fickle and capricious woman. He mentioned a place nearby. Instructed me to visit it. I understand it is a cemetery, or rather a catacomb. *Il Cimitero delle Fontanelle*. He has no inkling of what has brought me here. He said it's the most interesting place in the area. You can choose a skull and ask it what you like. He told me about a local family whose house was falling down. They went to see their skull and a few days later they found gold, a cascade of gold coins, inside a wall in their house. If I visit the cemetery, I'll go past the house; it's the nicest in the neighbourhood now. I won't, but I smile at the way life and death rub shoulders so openly here. The memento mori that pop up everywhere are nothing to do with grief or superstition: they are part of life.

I wonder why I am telling you all this. My thoughts are all over the place, I'm sure I'm boring you. The energy of this city and the change of scenery are such a welcome respite, I can forget about everything else. I'm writing to you as if I'd never lost you. Getting away from Paris, the hospital giving me a break from treatment, the sun, this habit I've developed of writing to you, it's all contributing to a lightness of being that I haven't felt for a long time. My dream is that when you read this letter, you will feel it too. Wouldn't it be wonderful if, absorbed in your reading, you too were suddenly taken by the illusion that this letter was only one of many: a normal letter, from a mother to her son, spending a few days apart. There is mercy in banality.

He

He didn't stop. An uninterrupted flow. Weeks went by. He stopped keeping count. Days merged into one another. Since the woman on the veranda, he'd been painting all the time. Today the woman was standing at the foot of a bed. The painting was almost finished. She held one hand to her belly. A rag doll hung from the other like a dead weight at the end of her arm. There was a small dog at her feet, yapping. She paid it no attention. Only the dog was moving. Perhaps it wanted to play, with her or with the doll, go outside and run round the garden in the background. But the woman stood stock still. Perhaps she was waiting for something.

He left the apartment as little as possible. Only the bare minimum: shopping, laundry, sometimes the café. It had been hot the last few days. He kept the windows open day and night. He ignored Marc's calls. He hadn't been in touch with Ariane; he wouldn't know what to say to her. She probably didn't really want to see him. He understood. It was a question of time. He didn't think about her very much. Like a distant memory. Almost another life. They would have to see each other at some point though. For her to look at the paintings. For the catalogue. He could leave the key under the doormat. She could come when he wasn't there. Her, alone, in the studio. He would go out. Would she agree? He'd received a third postcard from her. It was like a game now. This time she'd chosen an oil painting by Miró, with these words:

When, over deeps and deeps, a sun can pause
in the pure work of its eternal cause,
time flickers and the craving is to know.

Monsieur the Artist in reinforced cement, the next part lies dormant in 'The Graveyard by the Sea'.

He put down his paintbrush and poured the last drops of coffee into his cup. He'd had an ache in his lower back for the last few days. He slowly sipped the lukewarm coffee. He hadn't turned his most recent paintings to face the wall yet. They weren't dry. And they were still fresh in his mind as well. He contemplated them. The woman was always alone. As immobile as the objects surrounding her. She merged with them, as if they were a part of her. She stared into the distance, at something invisible. He'd given up trying to paint whatever it was. It was she who'd decided. He'd had to accept it, though he hadn't straightaway. He told himself he would see it at some point. But it was there. Her gaze remained fixed on the middle distance. Like the eyes of a blind woman. A woman who was looking from within and seeing beyond.

He took down from the shelf a book of poems that Ariane had given him early on in their relationship. He perched on the armrest and began to read. *The Graveyard by the Sea.* His vision grew blurred. The lines strained to make sense. He started again from the beginning, forced himself to focus. *The sea, the sea will always recommence!* He stopped and let the book fall back into his lap. He was eaten up with exhaustion. He ran a hand over the back of his neck. He'd take a shower in a bit. He tried to think back over the hours. He'd painted until very late, slept only a few hours. Yesterday? Or the day before? Working non-stop. He hadn't seen a soul. He might go mad, and he wouldn't even know it. In Mauritius he had friends, old school friends mainly. And ex-girlfriends. Whom he'd carried on seeing from time to time. Here he knew almost no one. He only talked to his paintings. He didn't mind. On the contrary. Even if it was a bottomless well reverberating with the infinite echo of his own voice. Back there, things had been simple. They hung out at the beach. Beer, barbecue. They went fishing. One of his friends ran a dive centre. He'd help him out in high season when he needed extra staff. Sometimes they went diving together. He didn't remember any one particular trip. They all merged into one. What came back to him was the weightlessness, the floating, far from everything, the dense silence cadenced by their slow breathing. He remembered the feeling of being submerged, the limitlessness, the intoxication of being absent from the world, of disappearing, and yet his heart beating more surely; elemental pleasure, the warm, liquid pouch of the ocean. He saw the path towards the light materialise as the water grew darker with each metre. And in the silence and the mystery, the beings that appeared, then grew indistinct and disappeared; their mouths that opened and closed; their mouths and the pulsation of their gills their sole impression on time and space. He saw the dance of the seven veils of the scorpion fish, the magnanimous race of the turtle, the furtive eye of the shark. He saw them as he saw things in a painting; an enhanced reality engulfing actual reality; and the way the soul expanded there.

Maybe one day he'd take Ariane to Mauritius. They would swim together. He had never seen her swim. He'd like to.

He shook himself awake from his reverie. He left the book of poems where it had fallen. He was starving. He decided to make some pasta with what was left in the fridge: a tomato and a piece of cheese. He cleared a corner of the table and sat down to eat, facing the window. On the other side of the courtyard, the window of the bedroom was open, the one that looked onto the bed. The woman lay on her side with her back to him. It was the first time he had seen her sleeping. She hadn't got under the sheets, had simply pulled a shawl over her legs. She was wearing a red dress in a pattern he couldn't quite make out. Her position accentuated the curve of her waist: a hollow before the rise of the hip. His eyes slid down to her bottom. He was surprised he didn't want to linger. He forced himself to. What was making him spy on this woman? He found a scrap of blank paper on the table and began to sketch. He drew the hollow of the mattress under the body, the head heavy on the pillow, the line of the neck abbreviated by the slight rise of the shoulder. One free arm disappearing towards the back of the room. A hand on top of the book that lay open beside her.

The sound of the phone startled him. Its ring bore into his skull. He got up quickly and lifted the receiver to make it stop. It was Marc.

'Goodness. It's vanishingly rare for you to pick up so quickly. For you to answer at all, in fact. Is everything okay?'

'Yes, yes.'

'What are you up to?'

'I'm painting.'

'Excellent. Shall I come over and distract you for a bit?'

'Aren't you away for the long weekend?'

'No, there was a mix-up.' (That would not have pleased Marc at all: empty diary, deserted Paris.) 'So, shall I come over?'

'Sure, come by if you like. I'm here.'

'Perfect. Let's have dinner. We can get a bite to eat somewhere near you.'

He didn't have time to answer: Marc had already hung up.

Marc blew in like the springtime: there he was, all at once, complete, and the air in the studio vibrated differently.

'Would you mind if I take a look around, now that I'm here?'

Had he come to see him or his work? The intrusion made him ill at ease.

'Go ahead, feel free. Since you're here.'

Marc began cautiously, then grew bolder. He shifted some of the paintings to get a better view, asked if he could bring out or turn round the ones that weren't displayed. He was calmly insistent. He didn't express an opinion, merely gave brief instructions: this one, that one, yes, a bit further, wait a minute, okay, no, the other one. Together they moved them, arranged them, rear-ranged them, rejected one, selected another. He simply complied as best he could, suddenly strangely awkward among his own canvases. It was only when Marc had gone through them all that the verdict was given:

'This is good. This is really good.'

He didn't know anymore. His visions had become corpses. He felt like he was suffocating. Had a sudden urge to be rid of them. To let Marc take them away, as quickly as possible.

'It's really you. The vegetation, the shadows, the enigma of it all, and then out of the blue, this woman. It's you and it's new. A few more canvases and we'll have an amazing show. There's nothing else to say: you've done it. Shall we go and eat?'

'I'm not very hungry, but okay. Give me a minute.'

He went to the bathroom and splashed his face in the sink. The cold water soothed his nerves. When he came out, Marc had stationed himself in front of the window.

'Do you know the people across the courtyard?'

'No, why?'

'Have you seen that babe on the right? Not bad, eh?'

He was appalled, at a loss for words.

'She's not young, but she's not bad at all. Have you ever seen her naked?'

Shut up.

'Do you want binoculars?'

'Do you have a pair?' An odious ghost of a smile.

'Stop it, Marc! Did you come here to ogle my neigh-bour or to do your job?'

'But I am doing my job: I'm immersing myself in the artist's world.'

'So stop looking over there: my paintings are in here, not on the other side of the courtyard.'

Marc stepped back from the window. He picked up a paintbrush and toyed with the bristles.

'Relax, man, I was just kidding. Out of the blue you've started painting all these women, I'm just looking for an explanation. Speaking of which – you never told me your mother died when you were a child.'

The words were like a punch in the stomach. Who had told him about his mother? The only person who knew was Ariane. He was dismayed.

'What the hell are you after exactly?'

Marc stiffened. 'I'm trying to understand.'

'Since when do you need to understand a picture to sell it?'

Curtly Marc put down the paintbrush and came and stood in front of him.

'Since always. Does it bother you?' His voice was composed and cold.

'Yes, it does bother me.'

'Really? Why?'

He was stuck, stupidly, with no idea what to say. Marc went on. 'Okay, I'm not going to ask you to explain, and I'm not going to try and figure it out on your behalf, but I am interested in you. I'm interested in you *and* your work. The two go together. Pending further instructions, you and your painting go together, alright?'

He was infuriated. He clenched his fists. A rage against the whole world, waiting to explode. He could have punched him. Marc didn't take his eyes off him.

'It's your quest, you do with it what you like. I'll take the lot: the misanthropic artist and his mysterious woman; your paintings and your pig-headedness. The extraordinary thing, if you really want to know, is that I already know it's going to be a sensation. I don't doubt it for a second. But for that to happen, you need to let me do my job. And what is my job? It's to help you.'

Disconcerted, he took a step back. His anger faltered. He was confused. The idea that someone wanted to help him seemed simultaneously sweet and suspect. He lowered his gaze. Sensing Marc's eyes on him, he stared even more intently at the floor, his jaw clenched.

'What more do you want me to say? That we're going to make a killing? It's not like you care about the money anyway.'

He relaxed his fists. Marc said jokingly, 'Don't worry though, we're still splitting it.' He put his hand on his arm. 'Come on, man, relax, this exhibition is going to be a dream.' He picked up the packet of cigarettes from the table.

'Mind if I have one?'

He nodded. Marc lit a cigarette, then started to rummage through the sheets of drawing paper on the table.

'I love your work and I believe in your talent. And I have done since the first day I discovered it in that hotel in Mauritius. Do you remember? I've never pretended otherwise. And because I love your bloody paintings, I want to champion them. Ariane too; you know that. So, for God's sake, have a bit of faith in us!'

It was the first time he'd seen Marc smoking. It was odd. He ran his hands over his face as if he was waking up. He relaxed his jaw and managed to mumble, 'I'm sorry.'

Marc sat down on the stool and crushed out his ciga-rette among the butts in the overflowing ashtray.

'No problem. You've been working like crazy; no wonder you're on edge. Don't worry about it.'

Marc had noticed that the stool turned like a screw, in both directions. Now he was having fun kicking his heels to make it spin round.

'Do you remember the gallerist from London I brought along to your show?'

'Vaguely.'

He swivelled round.

'Well, he'd like to meet you.'

Another swivel.

'Is he in Paris?'

Marc was starting to make him feel dizzy.

'No, in London, I told you. He's planning an exhi-bition of young up-and-coming French artists. The sooner you go over to remind him of your existence, the better.'

'To London?'

'Yes, it's only a Eurostar away and it'll be a nice change of scene for you.'

He caught sight of his reflection in the window. His eye sockets made two black holes in his face. He looked slightly mad. He hadn't shaved for days, he'd barely washed. Drooping shoulders. Old T-shirt. Hair stick-ing up. Feral, like a cat.

'London. Not sure that's a good idea.'

'On the contrary, it's an excellent idea; in fact, I've already bought your ticket.' He leaped to his feet. 'Shall we go and eat?'

She

I've been sleeping more and more. Fatigue is stealing too much of my cherished time. It didn't used to seem so precious, until it started to run out. Now I have started this work, I'd like to see it through properly. Monologue is a more difficult exercise than conversation. If you could talk back to me, I would have a better idea of what to say.

Should I tell you about the years that followed your disappearance? I imagine you'd like to know. It is so much and so little. My pen baulks. I am still not sure. Will telling you about myself make you fixate on retracing my life? I think that would be dangerous and pointless. You'll argue that I've already entrusted you with this Pandora's box by writing this letter. I grant that. But even if the truth is healthy, an obsession with the past is dangerous. If you keep looking back, you can't walk straight, and then you might fall. I don't have much time left. You do. I want you to see things clearly and keep looking straight ahead. Don't delve more deeply than these lines I've written. That would be a project without end. A state of mourning beyond your reach. I hope this letter will impel you towards the future. Don't try to revive the past. Don't go looking for the people I used to know. You'd like someone to tell you about me? Tell yourself that nobody knew me. I hid from everyone.

How I hated the precautions people used to

take to avoid mentioning children around me. I began to avoid anyone who knew the story of your disappearance. I learnt not to talk about it to anyone I met after it happened. I learnt to keep relationships superficial. Paradoxically, I didn't want to make your abduction the focal point of my life in other people's eyes, so I never talked about it. I didn't want to be defined by your absence, precisely because I was filled with you. No one would have understood. The consequence was that anyone who tried to get close to me was always missing the thing that mattered most. I'd let them tiptoe around me, I managed to fool them, but nobody could get through to who I really was.

I pieced myself back together, slowly and differently. To this day, I still don't know how I was able to do it. Working was what helped me the most.

Originally – you might not know this – I trained as a pharmacist. For a few months after you disappeared, I carried on working at the pharmacy, and then one morning I didn't go in. It was a pure instinct for survival. It would have been so easy to open a drawer and take what I needed to end the awful pain. But I had to live. I owed it to you, for the slim chance that I might see you again one day. It became obvious that my only option was to reinvent myself.

I wanted to go back to university, but I couldn't afford it. I went to see my parents and asked them to lend me the money. It cost me dear to ask them. They were so in thrall to their bourgeois values they were barely able to listen to me, they couldn't understand at all. I enrolled in college. History was an obvious choice, art a magnet. That's how I became a museum guide. Please don't imagine I was some kind of bluestocking or a sour old maid. I learned to love life again, rediscovered an appetite for many things, beauty above all. Art saved me.

It started with the thrill of studying. I was older than the other students. Because of that, and all the rest, I was a little bit of an outsider. This was good for me: there weren't so many distractions, which meant I worked harder. I was happy to lose myself in books. That was all I wanted. Reality was intolerable, so the unreality of art became my refuge. There was no room for emptiness in this dream. It fulfilled me. In this new life, my blood hadn't been spilled. It was just that it was hard to live two lives at once: one concrete and mechanical, the other warm and inhabited. I came back to myself in this dreamscape, slipping out of this world and into art as you might dive into a warm lake. I took off my dark clothes and dived into the water, immersed myself completely, eyes wide open, and let myself be consoled.

Works of art were better at coaxing out the right words. Learning to love people again was not so easy.

He

He was woken up by a passenger announcement. On the other side of the glass the landscape had changed. Hedges, farms, road markings. England. The train must have gone through the tunnel while he was sleeping. He looked at his watch. About twenty minutes to go before they got to London. He opened the book he'd brought with him. An essay that Ariane had given him when she'd come to the studio a few days before. He grinned at the recollection.

'This is a purely professional appointment,' she'd said when she arrived. 'About the introduction for your catalogue.'

She wore a skirt that clung to her waist and hips. When she stood in front of the easel with her back to him, he couldn't take his eyes off her bottom. He tried to stay focused.

It was the first time she'd seen the paintings, but she didn't pick him up on it. He was grateful. He could have told her that her opinion counted more than anyone else's, but he decided it wasn't necessary, she must have known.

Without turning round, she said, 'Stop looking at me like that. You're making it impossible for me to concentrate on your work.'

He went and stood by the window and lit a cigarette. He broke two matches before he managed it. He stayed there, looking out of the window, but he couldn't filter out Ariane's presence as she scrutinised his paintings. He listened out for a sigh, an exclamation, anything. He couldn't stand it any longer.

'So, what do you think?'

'Shush,' she answered.

She came towards him, placed her hand on his cheek and forced him to turn his face towards her. She held his gaze. Slowly her hand slid along his jaw until she placed a finger on his lips. Her touch was like an electric shock. She repeated:

'Shush.'

He could feel her breath. Suddenly he felt as shy as a child. He knew she understood him. She smiled. She might as well make the most of having come. Fair game.

She undid the buttons of his shirt one by one, ran her hands over his chest. He didn't move, just trembled slightly. She continued to undress him. He let her. Still she didn't speak. She took off her T-shirt and slipped out of her skirt. In a moment she was standing against him, completely naked. Very delicately he took her face in his hands, raised it towards him and put his lips on her magnificent smile. He carried her over to the bed and as he entered her, the world faded away, dissolving into a calm, warm ocean.

Later, as night fell, coming back to reality, she announced with a mischievous laugh:

'So now I'll be able to tell you what I think of your paintings. And you'll be able to listen to me!'

She talked for a long time. He didn't interrupt. She was discerning about what really mattered; what she held back was testimony to her tact and respect. He was profoundly moved to hear his visions put into words by

Ariane, the way they came out of her mouth and were returned to him, illuminated. She gave them back to him in an intelligible form. Now he was able to gauge their meaning. All those months of pain and uncertainty hadn't been in vain. He had made it possible for other people to see, feel, understand a truth which exceeded him.

In the train bearing him away from Paris he could still feel Ariane's lips and in this intimacy the power of a profound truth, discovered and shared.

Before he left, she said to him, 'I'm going to write the introduction, you're going to do your exhibition, and afterwards the two of us are going to have to talk.'

She

I really don't want you to think I was unhappy or isolated. I have never been lonely. This will surprise you, but even after you'd gone, you never stopped bringing me countless little moments of joy.

I'd be leafing through a book, and a line would make me smile and, in my head, I'd share it with you. In the local park, I'd look at the children and feel proud of the person I knew you had become. At the museum, I sometimes gave tours to school groups. Their enthusiasm, candour and cheekiness always made me smile. I celebrated every one of your birthdays in secret. It was never a sad day. I was filled with happiness that you were growing up. Every year I imagined you a little changed, a little older, maybe even more handsome. All I wanted was for you to be happy. Whenever I thought about you, I was sure that wherever you were, you would sense this, and know how much I loved you.

You taught me to love. Even the horror of your absence could not take this gift away from me. By keeping you close to me, I managed to carry on loving. How can I explain this?

I remember going to visit a colleague one day. She had a son about your age. This little boy, who would have been about ten at the time, sat with us reading a comic. His presence, far from being distressing, was a delight. I couldn't stop looking at him. When

I got up to go, I ran my fingers through his hair, ruffling it affectionately the way adults often do to children. As I touched his hair a tremendous rush of happiness and gratitude came over me. The feeling was so strong that tears came to my eyes. Not tears of sadness, I promise you, but of elation. Somewhere, I also had a son. Another cherub like this one, living and growing, reading comics with delicious concentration, alongside two ladies drinking tea and chatting, rewarding them with his indifference, quite oblivious to how much he was admired and loved. Do you understand what I'm trying to say? Without you, I wouldn't have been able to feel this great surge of love. It's your existence that gave me this capacity to appreciate and feel emotion, so powerful and intimate.

Of course, sometimes your absence was unbearable. I lost hope. Your image grew hazy, as if you were slipping away. Those days were dreadful. I didn't know how to reach you or where to find you. Life made no sense. Everything I had constructed seemed to be in vain. Maybe you weren't how I imagined you. Maybe you were dead. Maybe I was clinging to a chimera. But on days when I had faith, nothing weighed on me, because you were with me. If you grew up without a mother, if no woman ever took my place, know that you did have one, even if you never knew. I never stopped seeing you, marvelling at you, talking to you. The only thing that was denied me was your physical presence. *Noli me tangere*. But just as one can believe without seeing, one can also love without touching.

He

He got off the train and the flood of passengers bore him down into the bowels of the station. He bought a map and located the Underground. In the corridors and then on the Tube he was struck by the colours, more vivid and varied than in Paris. Things, people. The absence of familiar smells. The movement too: faster, more controlled. Synchronised. Like figure skating. In Paris, by contrast, the Metro was like an anthill that someone had kicked over.

For once, he was in plenty of time. He decided to get off one station early, at Piccadilly Circus, the only name on the line that meant anything to him. The crowd steered him up to the surface. A great wave. Marc was right. A change of scene was good for him. He breathed more easily. He looked at everything with the eyes of a child. The city seeped into his pores. Brought him out of himself. He turned down side streets at random to avoid the tourists. There seemed to be a lot of office blocks. In vast marble and glass lobbies, reception-ists greeted men in well-cut suits with professional smiles. Everyone walked with a determined air. He let himself be carried along, a stowaway. He glanced at his watch. He was quite capable of missing his appoint-ment. Another couple of hours to kill. He patted the map in his pocket. He would use it if he had to, but for the time being he was savouring the freedom. The city demanded nothing of him.

At the end of a sunless alleyway, he found himself in a massive square, bounded on one side by a magnificent edifice. 'National Gallery', he read on the facade. How funny, Ariane had told him about it. He was pretty sure she had. He decided to go in and look around.

The museum was huge. He wandered through it with no particular purpose. Moved quickly through the first galleries without paying much attention, more interested in the atmosphere and the visitors. There were a lot of tourists and the odd group of uniformed schoolchildren. He never felt comfortable in museums. In Paris, it took all of Ariane's cajoling to get him inside one. He contemplated leaving. Being here alone was a waste of time. He wasn't in the right frame of mind for a lesson in art history. Nonetheless, gradually, the paintings and sculptures began to draw him in. He recognised several from reproductions he'd seen in books. He slowed his pace, to pause in front of one or another. Even read some of the labels. Every so often he sat down on a bench to spend time with a painting, to decrypt it, drink in every detail. He stopped in a gallery of portraits from the Italian Renaissance: a young poet with dreamy eyes, a man, possibly a banker, with a resolute air, another holding a letter, and then an older man clutching a book. He noted a tension around the eyes, an angle of the wrist, the nap of a velvet coat. All these figures holding onto their secrets were extraordinarily present. He looked closely at each one, walked back and forth between them, as if he were verifying something. But then a sickening sensation came over him. Why were they all looking at him like that? What was the point of continuing to exist like that? How ridiculous they were, trapped inside their frames, pretending they still had something to say. Let's face it, they were all dead, like everyone is in the end. He wanted them all to shut up. To shut up, to put an end to the whole damn thing! He rushed out of the gallery and bumped into a guard, who gave him a dirty look. He walked fast, trying to find the exit, but he couldn't see a sign. The rooms jumped from one historical period to another. Southern Europe. Northern Europe. One Old Master after another. He walked past bodies and faces, an indigestible chaos. He saw Botticelli, Cranach, almost stopped in front of Titian. He ignored Rubens. Too much flesh. All he wanted was to get out. To escape from the pressure choking him. He felt sweat beading on his forehead. It was so hot in the museum. He was short of breath. His eyes grew dim. He saw a bench, hurried towards it, and sank onto it.

It would pass. He took off his jacket. He was just going to have to sit it out, head in hands, eyes closed. Paintings danced before him like visions. Muddled details appeared. The fold of a sleeve. The stroke of a brush. A shiver. He saw each painter harnessed to his task. He felt the weight of the palette in their hands, the pressure of the brush against the canvas, its tip loaded with paint. Shapes blurred. He was overwhelmed by the jumble of shadows and hues, and all the people he could sense around him, a crowd of artists, each standing in front of a canvas. He was one of them. One among thousands of painters. He belonged to their mad brotherhood. Yes, he was like them. Crazy like them. Determined to coax something out – he didn't even know what. He didn't ask himself. All he knew was loneliness, permanent dissatisfaction, relentlessness, the rage of impotence, the perpetual lack of fulfilment, the unceasing restlessness in his soul. All this effort, just to experience for a brief moment the impression of having grasped something. Of having bestowed meaning. Of having tried. Whatever it took to survive. Yes, this was his family: the restless, the possessed, the obstinate. People who sketch, strike through, create, destroy, and start again, endlessly, in search of some truth. Some goddamn truth that might not even really exist.

He looked up at the painting in front of him. It was Rembrandt, a late self-portrait. Drooping features, hands crossed one over the other. No brush or palette. Assured and serene. He had said all that he had to say. He had nothing more to prove to himself. He was beyond all that. Was such a thing possible? Could one really attain that? That calm. His expression was so gentle. He imagined him painting his reflection in a mirror. How had he managed to see himself so clearly? And suddenly he understood that Rembrandt wasn't speaking for himself. He wasn't delivering a mono-logue. He was offering himself for others to see. He was offering us his eyes, other eyes. It was a gift of self, a shared experience of being. His throat tightened. He wanted to embrace this man, to thank him, to love him like a father.

He took the book Ariane had given him out of his pocket. He'd turned down the corner of a page this morning in the train. He found the passage: 'Without honesty, there is no possible universality, human and alive. The eye of the painter seeks genuine interiority.

Not the interior of other things, but its own interiority, projected onto them. He is inviting the viewer to do the same. The exacting mirror of the painter is simultaneously turned towards himself and towards the other.'

He thought of what Marc had said. 'I'm immersing myself in the artist's world.' Marc was wrong to look for the explanation of his paintings in the outside world. It was somewhere else. It was in the interior magma he'd let himself slip into. A different reality, accessible only through this other language. A living language, specifically human – that of painting, music, all the arts. With no restrictions, no taboo, no limit other than that imposed by honesty. He was talking to himself, but not completely alone. A soliloquy. Turning inwards, but addressing everyone. Unafraid to fling the curtains wide open, because it wasn't narcissism. It wasn't self-love. It wasn't even an excuse to pretend to be moving from the particular to the universal. It was a compulsion, a human necessity. The respiration of the great interior chaos of the human – without which we aren't truly alive. It has to be offered up with an open heart, so that others can take possession of it. That was the reason he painted. Nothing else had any meaning, any value. This was the only true thing he was capable of.

He closed the book. With one last look, he thanked Rembrandt and resumed his walk through the galleries. Behind each work stood a man, artist or craftsman, a brother. All, like him, killing themselves to tell their truth. He wasn't alone. He was filled with blazing conviction. He was right to be trying. He was sure of it.

Absorbed in thought, he must have missed the sign for the exit. The place was a warren. He found himself in a smaller, dimly lit gallery, with fewer pictures and no way through. He was about to turn round when a painting caught his eye.

It wasn't very big. It showed a couple standing in a bedchamber. It was an oddly familiar image. Of course, it was well-known, but that wasn't it. He peered at the label: Jan van Eyck, 'The Arnolfini Portrait', 1434. He instinctively disliked their rigid pose and tight little smiles. He wasn't keen on Flemish painting. So what was it that held his attention? Was it the convex mirror that hung between them, like the one in Jeune Vieille's apartment? He looked from the man to the woman. How horribly stiff they both were. On the floor, trapped between them, their tense, sad little dog didn't seem any more alive than they. He'd have liked to pick up the little dog and pull it out of the painting, bring it back to life. And the woman as well, to take her hand away from the man's, to protect her from the fatal contact. The sweet young bride, the heavy folds of her dress draped over her swollen belly. She was soon to be a mother.

And still he stood there, searching – the way the fabric fell, the two faces, the bed, the mirror, the shaggy little dog, the strange sandals, the window, the chandelier – for the solution to an unintelligible mystery. He came up against the man's severity, the woman's reserve, the deceptive, unnatural tranquillity of the scene. It made him think of the eye of a cyclone. Everything had been blown away, except this room. He peered at the mirror. A half-open door and two figures reflected in it. It made no sense. It should have been the painter and his easel. He struggled with this incongruity. He wanted to understand. What was the painter's intention? It was clear that there was something concealed in the miniature reflection. He stared at the distorted image. He forgot he was standing in the gallery of a museum. He was lost in the image, in the mirror; he was on the other side, in that hazy bubble, peering through the half-open door.

When he surfaced from his reverie, he promised himself he'd buy a postcard of the painting on his way out so he could continue trying to figure it out, but he forgot.

She

I don't think I'll be coming out of hospital. My strength is ebbing away, and with it the likelihood of seeing you. The dark shadow that clouds my thoughts is not so much the illness, but the thought of not seeing you again.

This afternoon I am going to ask someone to deliver this letter to your grandmother. The chances are minimal, but it's the only link with you I have left. If ever one day you were to reappear, the trail would certainly lead you to her. I have barely seen her since the event. The investigation obliged us to stay in contact for a while. Then the relationship became more tenuous. I used to call her from time to time, always hoping she would finally have some news of your father and you.

I'd never felt close to her, and your disappearance didn't change that. In fact it was the opposite. I found it too painful to see her, precisely because it felt so pointless. We both suffered from the same absence – after all she had lost her son too. But it was no use. Everyone reacts to grief in their own way.

I didn't blame her for her coldness. I tried to pierce its mystery. It must have had its roots in the convergence of character with upbringing. Was it marriage that had imposed such a hard-hearted facade on her? Your grandfather was an army general. I never met him. He died before your father and

I married, but he often came up in conversation, and it was as if the portrait in the living room still stood in glacial judgement over everything. Did your grandmother also suffer? Does she still? Keeping things and people at a distance is a way of protecting oneself. My heart wants to excuse this woman. I don't know if I should trust her. Your father seemed to love her, in his own way. He had great respect for her. I don't want to believe that her severity contributed to your father's inflexibility. It's so easy to blame the mother.

Sometimes, fleetingly, I was convinced I'd caught a gleam in her eye, a loosening of her lips, a suppressed elation. There was this strange moment in the maternity ward after your birth. She slipped her finger into your little hand. Your tiny fingers squeezed it and she smiled in a way I had never seen before. She looked at you with an expression of unadulterated love, bright rays pouring out over the promise you represented. But after you disappeared, what of that could possibly have remained?

So when the search for you was eventually called off, I had no reason, besides loyalty, to carry on seeing her. I tried to maintain the relationship for a while, but it was beyond me. Deep down, I wonder if your grandmother never really forgave me. Just as I was tempted to hold her responsible, I suspect that she wanted to believe I was the guilty party. I had rejected her son. That in itself, for any mother, is unpardonable. This on top of the fact that obedience to certain principles, whatever the cost, was for her an ineluctable value. Her whole life was based on blind respect for authority, whether male or divine. She must have sacrificed a great deal of herself on that altar. Understanding my behaviour would have meant renouncing who she was: my defiance was dangerously disruptive and needed to be held in check. I was a virus, contaminating and threatening, from which she had to protect herself. That is what I always sensed I was to her: an undesirable element.

In spite of everything, here I am reduced to entrusting this woman with the possibility of us meeting again someday. It's better than not trying at all. We won't be reunited in the flesh, it will be in these pages. It is not much, I know. So many times I've dreamed I was holding you in my arms. All I clutched was emptiness. I am enraged we haven't found each other. The thought of you holding these few sheets of paper instead of being able to hug you makes me want to scream, to abandon the whole thing. Yet even after all this time, I won't accept that you were deprived of my love. It is intact, abundant, infinite. It has never been dented. It's been sustained all these years, and it still burns, deep within me, as intensely as ever. I hope these pages offer you some comfort.

No child was ever more loved than you.

He

His trip to London was like a window opening in a room that had been sealed shut for too long. When he got back to Paris he began painting with renewed energy. He didn't judge or try to understand what the woman was doing there. He accepted her as one accepts the fact of having two legs and two arms. He painted her like he breathed, without thinking about it. And she stayed with him, on the canvas, without moving.

Glorious rays of July sunlight fell across the floor. Cheerful Saturday morning music drifted up from the courtyard. He felt a sudden desire to see Ariane. Where had she got to with the catalogue? She hadn't talked to him about it at all. A young man had come to photograph the paintings. That was all he knew. Why didn't she feel the need to discuss things with him, to shed light on certain things? Maybe she thought she knew him well enough. He put on a shirt, glanced in the bathroom mirror. He couldn't find a comb, so he ran his fingers impatiently through his hair and left the apartment.

He walked out of the Metro station and picked up some croissants. The air was crystalline and warm; he stretched like a tiger. Summer in Paris was so different to what he was used to. He went into a café and drank a quick espresso at the bar. He paid and walked across the square. The monochrome blue sky swathed it in a smooth, flat tint. He went through the door of Ariane's apartment building and hurried up the stairs, running his hand along the banister. The wood was warm to the touch and slightly tacky. There was the smell of beeswax in the air. Outside her door he stopped to catch his breath. The building was silent. He put his finger to the bell, strangely hesitant. He didn't know why. It was ridiculous. He'd come; he was there; he wasn't going to turn around now. He wanted to know where she was with the catalogue. He rang the bell. He waited. No sound. No answer. Except for his pounding heart. He tried to remember if Ariane had mentioned a trip, a weekend away, anything. He looked at his finger on the doorbell. His fingernail was encrusted with dried paint. He looked up. The fanlight in the roof over the staircase framed the sky, the same limpid blue.

He thought of the early morning sky when he used to run down to the beach to swim. He went swimming before his father woke up, in the boundless space of the dawn. He felt the tingle, the taste of the salt. The waves held him, cradled him. He closed his eyes.

A sound brought him back to himself. Someone on one of the floors below, going down the stairs. Rapid footsteps, all the way down, the murmur of the street and the heavy door banging shut. Then silence. In front of him, Ariane's door, like a wall. He was seized by impatience. He rang the bell again. Held his finger down. He would count to ten. At ten, he'd release his finger. He counted very slowly to ten. Lifted his finger, still hopeful. The door didn't open. His fist tightened. He raised it and slammed the wood, hard. Then again. He hammered at the door, again and again, until it hurt. Until he felt ashamed of his absurd behaviour.

Out on the street he threw the croissants into a bin. He headed towards Saint-Germain, turned onto the rue du Four until he reached the rue de Seine. He knew the gallery would be closed at this hour. He stopped in front of it. In the window were some sculptures by an artist he vaguely knew. They'd met a few times. He remembered him. Marc had introduced them. A gentle, self-effacing man. When you met him, you couldn't possibly imagine any of this: the gashes, the twisted limbs, the jagged bronze. In a little more than a month, his own wounds were going to be displayed here for all to see. The exhibitionism disgusted him.

He didn't start working when he got home. He sat down in the armchair. The woman across the courtyard wasn't there. Her bedroom was empty. He looked at the desk, the chair, the candle, and other things as well – a cup, the whorls on the rug, a lithograph on the wall. There was a book on the table by her bed. He went to find his binoculars.

He wasn't a voyeur, he just wanted to look at the book, simple curiosity. That was all. She wasn't there. He adjusted the focus. The window, the wall, the bed, the book. He tried to read the title. He braced his elbows on the windowsill. Adjusted the binoculars again. Nothing to be done. The lettering was too small.

But really, after all, what did he care what the woman was reading? The image of Ariane's closed door came back to him. He could still taste his bitter disappointment. Why was he missing her now? He mustn't blow it out of proportion.

He was in the middle of a painting. It was going to be a central piece in the exhibition. The composition had come to him out of the blue. He hadn't been thinking about it, it just came. It was smaller than usual. A woman, from behind, looking into a mirror. One of her hands pressed against it, as if against a windowpane. His paintbrush forged a path. The woman's reflection gradually emerged. Her face materialised as if being drawn out of a long sleep. Like a statue fished from the bottom of the ocean. Her eyes were dark, her lips half-open. The paintbrush conjured the subject. Her skin thickened, grew warm. He could smell and hear her. He forgot everything else. He forgot he was painting. The easel, the canvas, time itself no longer existed. He was voice and touch, flesh and dreams. He was this mouth uttering long-forgotten words. A door swung open. The woman, affectionate and at peace, saw him at last in the mirror's reflection.

She

How to end this, if I don't accept there is an ending? Please tell me this isn't one. Tell me these words go even a tiny way towards filling the void. I can't bear to think of you sad, or enslaved by anger. Know this: bitterness is a terrible companion. These pages won't give you back your mother. They cannot put things right. And yet. At least you know a bit more about me now. I feel as though we've spent some time together. What's the expression? 'Out of sight, out of mind'? Not true for a mother. I love you still, despite everything, beyond anything, unconditionally and absolutely. We are the proof, you and I, that love, no slave to time, scoffs at separation.

He

Marc was putting the pressure on him now. 'This is the last lap, man. There's a real buzz around the show. I've got a feeling it's going to be a big hit. You've put your heart and soul into these paintings.' Perhaps that was true. He felt utterly drained.

The studio was bathed in September light. He knelt down on the floor to unroll a length of bubble wrap. Traces of his toil everywhere: splashes of paint, some still fresh. The pictures had already gone to the gallery, apart from the one with the mirror that he was holding onto until the last minute. Was Marc right? He thought about the pieces: how he'd painted them, the hours it had taken, the doubts. What was it worth, all that? He hadn't expected anything; he'd just been trying things out. He'd taken a risk. Pushed himself as far as he could. Tried to say something. Mind you, even though the show was opening the next day, even though this phase was over, he knew he was going to have to keep going, even further. He had to keep searching. For what, he had no idea. Would he ever?

The woman in the mirror stared back at him, her hand reaching out to touch him, stopped by the mirror. He picked up the painting and laid it gently on the plastic. *Come on, let's get you to the gallery. It's time.* He knelt over the portrait, stared at her for a moment, then folded the plastic over her. Her face grew blurred. When he stood up, he almost lost his balance. What an idiot! He could have destroyed it.

As he was leaving the apartment, the painting under his arm, the telephone rang. He hesitated, glancing at his watch, then picked up the receiver, thinking it might be the gallery.

'Hallo?' It was Geneviève. Damn. He didn't have time for this right now.

'You need to come and see me.'

He could hardly make out the old lady's voice. This was the first time she'd ever called him. It was strange to hear her voice without being able to see her face. She sounded like she was fighting for breath.

'Can it wait? My exhibition opens tomorrow night.'

'No. You must come. I'm in the hospital.'

He put down the painting.

'What happened?' The old lady didn't answer. All he heard was her rasping breath and the sound of a machine in the background. 'Okay then, tell me which hospital you're in.' She mumbled a name. He vaguely knew where it was. He looked at his watch again and thought for a moment. 'I'll come straightaway.'

On the other end of the line he heard, as though from very far away, 'That's good. I'm waiting for you.'

He'd go to the hospital on the way to the gallery. The painting wasn't heavy. He checked the route on a map, to be sure. As he was folding it up, he automatically cast a glance out of the window. The woman still wasn't home. It had been several days now.

He picked up the painting and left.

The hospital was buzzing with activity. The painting was cumbersome. Someone pointed him in the right direction. Old buildings alternated with modern ones that needed a coat of paint. People, noises muffled and shrill, strip lights. He quickened his step. He found the room. He knocked and entered. The old lady lay propped up in bed, an oxygen mask over her nose, her eyes turned towards him. He was taken aback by her hollow cheeks. He leaned the painting against the wall and went over to the bed. She pulled off the mask with difficulty. Her emaciated fingers were like spider legs.

'There you are.' She spoke with a weak rasp. 'What have you brought with you?' She pointed to the package.

'A painting.' Her hand fell back on the sheet. 'What's the matter, Geneviève?'

'The end.' She coughed. 'I'm almost at the end.'

'Don't say that.'

She gestured to him to sit down.

'It's a good thing you came.' She gasped for breath as she spoke. 'There are things one has to do.' Her voice grew faint. 'Face judgement.'

She was seized by another coughing fit. He filled the glass on the table and handed it to her. She tried to drink. He got up to help but didn't know how to do it properly. Water dribbled from the corner of her mouth onto the sheet.

'Because of certain things. Serious things. The Lord knows.'

He sat down again. The painting of the woman wrapped in plastic was leaning against the wall behind him. He looked at his watch.

'Geneviève, I'm sorry, I don't have much time.' He couldn't look at her as he said this.

'Neither do I.'

'Are you in pain? Shall I talk to the doctors?'

'Leave the doctors alone.'

He knew Marc would be at the gallery, pacing up and down, on edge. He repeated that he couldn't stay long today because of the exhibition, but he'd come back, maybe not tomorrow, but the day after. In reality, there wasn't much left to do. The exhibition was ready, but he couldn't focus on anything else. It wasn't the right time. His mind was elsewhere. This was too much to deal with right now.

She lifted her hand and pointed to an envelope on the bedside table. 'Take that and go.' She pursed her lips, whether with sadness or disgust he couldn't tell. 'Yes, it's for you. The Lord is calling me. Come along, take it.' He did so. As he picked up the envelope, he felt the old lady's fingers on his hand. He was surprised by how warm they felt. 'But wait until I'm dead. Not long now. Then you can open it. Do you hear me? Only then.'

He took the envelope. There was nothing written on it. He thought fleetingly of asking her what was in it. 'Did you hear me?' she repeated.

'What?'

'I'm asking you not to open it before.'

'Don't talk like that, Geneviève. It's going to be fine, you'll see.'

He stood up. 'Are you sure there's nothing I can do for you?' He slipped his hand into his pocket. He hesitated for a moment, then drew out an invitation card for the exhibition and handed it to her.

'Here. You won't make it to the opening, of course, but maybe later on. It'll be on for a while.'

She'd gone very pale. Silence filled the room.

'Yes, of course. Later on. My darling.'

He walked over to the bed to say goodbye, but he didn't know how. He stood there as if paralyzed.

'I am at peace now. I have done what I had to do. I shall keep praying for you from up there.'

She grasped the mask and clumsily placed it back on her face. He put the envelope down on the bed to help her fit it on properly and open the oxygen valve. With one finger, she pushed the letter towards him. He took it – for her, not for him. If it was a will, he wasn't interested. A souvenir of his father? He certainly didn't want that. What was it? He didn't want to know. He picked up the painting and tucked it under his arm. At the doorway, he turned one last time. The old lady's eyes were fixed on him. She didn't seem such a stranger anymore.

Out in the corridor, he took a deep breath. He walked past closed doors and then stood motionless waiting for the lift. He drew himself in, made way, slipped past. After the exit, on the other side of the metal railings, he stopped for a moment, adjusted the painting and the envelope, contemplated lighting a cigarette, sighed deeply, then made his way towards the Metro.

In the packed carriage, he forced himself not to think. He had to save his strength. He tried to slip the envelope into his pocket, but it didn't fit. He got off the train.

He walked. His mind failed to generate any clear thoughts. His back was hunched over. By the time he pushed open the door of the gallery he looked like a bull entering the ring.

'Ah, there you are!' He was stopped dead by Marc's embrace. 'What do we have here? The pièce de résistance?'

He tried, in vain, to keep hold of the painting, but Marc took it from him and tore off the bubble wrap. The woman emerged. Marc carried her to the back of the gallery and hung her on the only remaining blank wall.

'Et voilà, the family is complete!' He stepped back to admire the effect. 'A triumph, I'm telling you. We've got a hit on our hands!'

He looked at Marc, then at his paintings, incredulous. He saw them through a dense fog. The forms and the colours rippled. They began a slow, enigmatic dance. The women were floating and turning, and he was caught in the current. He tried to fix his gaze on one point, any point, to keep his balance, but the images were too indistinct. He could just make out the mirror, a phosphorescent portal. The light was unbearable. He closed his eyes.

'Are you okay?' Marc's hand on his arm. 'You've gone all pale; what's wrong? I hope you're not going to be ill just before the show opens. Come and sit down. What's in the envelope?'

He clutched the envelope tightly to his body. He struggled to remember. 'It's nothing. An old lady who's in hospital.'

Marc sat him down in his office. 'Someone close?'

'No, nobody close.'

'Is there anything I can do?'

'No.'

Marc handed him a glass of water. 'You look absolutely terrible. Why don't you go home and take a rest? You can see we're all set here. Take this box of invites, if you've got any last-minute guests.' He handed him a little box. On the lid, the woman in the mirror was watching him.

He made his way home on automatic pilot. As he approached his apartment building, he had an idea. Instead of going inside, he carried on down the block and round the corner until he arrived at a portico. He went inside, for the first time. The hallway was dark, flanked by a long wall of mailboxes. He peered at the unfamiliar names, hoping for a clue. He found none. He opened the box of invitation cards and counted them. Twenty-eight, that would be enough. He carefully posted a card into each slot. Then he went home.

He picked up another postcard from Ariane. Just these words, in her tall, sloping hand:

But grant that light must trace
half shadows in its ever-bleaker shade.

He'd see her tomorrow at the opening. He slipped the postcard into his coat pocket and walked up to his apartment. He realised he was still holding the envelope the old lady had given him. He placed it on the windowsill and wriggled his fingers, a bit stiff from clutching it so tightly. His eyes were drawn to the other side of the courtyard. Her windows were dark. He hoped she would come.

Epilogue

The gallery was buzzing. He shook hands, embraced strangers, smiled back. The crowd stood between him and his paintings. He'd have preferred everyone to turn and look at them instead of him. They knew, he didn't. The only thing he knew how to do was paint. And yet he was the one facing a barrage of questions. *Why this change of direction? Why an ever-present female figure after landscapes empty of any human presence? Is this a logical continuation of your earlier work? Is she an incarnation of the natural world? Is Mauritius still present in your work, or should this series be considered a Parisian series? Are you exploring the female condition? Loneliness? The human condition?* He didn't have any answers, all he could offer was scattered, random thoughts. He talked about the multifaceted, elusive woman. He talked about the thing she was looking at, but which remained untouchable, beyond the frame. He kept casting his glance towards the gallery entrance. *Who is this woman?* He had no idea what to say. *And what about the mirror, the focal point of the exhibition?*

Marc was in his element, playing the host with brio.

'Let me introduce you to Monsieur C., a very important Swiss collector and, if I may be so bold, a faithful friend of the gallery.' He turned to Monsieur C. 'I understand you're quite taken with the woman in the mirror.' The Swiss man had a jovial face and a firm handshake.

He pictured the woman hanging in a large living room above a marble-inlaid console table. He took a gulp of champagne that went down the wrong way, and turned away to cough.

Next Marc led him over to a journalist. 'Do you remember Madame L.? She wrote a marvellous review of your first exhibition.'

The woman was tall and distinguished looking. She took his hand in hers.

'I'm not going to let you go. I must have an interview. Are you free tomorrow?'

'Yes, tomorrow's fine.' He glanced towards the door again. Still nothing.

He caught a glimpse of Ariane in the throng of people. She grinned at him. Her smile was like an outstretched hand. He wanted to grab hold of her. He smiled back. He was pleased she was there.

'Was this one inspired by Dalí's portrait of Gala?'

'No, I don't think so, no,' he stammered. 'But there's a Flemish painting...'

His voice was lost in the hubbub. Questions assailed him like a swarm of wasps. *Who are your influences? Have you any idea what you might do next? Who was your model? Is she here? You were saying?* The threads of all the different conversations fused into an amorphous, self-spawning mass. He stopped paying attention, offered only the vaguest answers. All these people suddenly seemed like puppets on a distant stage, performing a play for him, the sole spectator. He thought of his studio. That was where he wanted to be. He hankered after the feeling of the brush in his hand, the dialogue with the canvas, the silence. He craved simple, honest forms. He kept glancing occasionally towards the door, but now he knew she wouldn't come. Maybe she didn't really exist, maybe he had only imagined her. He felt a sudden sense of hopelessness. And yet – all these people, tonight – was this real or a dream? In which of these two spaces did he exist? Was he no more than an intermediary, a messenger between two worlds?

Gradually the gallery emptied out. Ariane had to go; she had dinner plans. He thanked her for coming. She made him promise they would see each other soon. 'Now that you've pulled it off,' she said. It was like a door was opening again. He looked around for Marc and spotted him in a corner, all smiles, deep in conversation with a woman. He decided not to interrupt him, said goodbye to a couple of people he knew among the stragglers, and slipped away.

He went home alone, on foot. The air smelled of the changing season. He was tired. He wanted a cigarette. As he took the packet from his pocket, he found Ariane's most recent postcard. He hadn't paid proper attention to it. This time there was no picture. Only a quotation, printed in oblique letters on a white background:

The wind is rising! ... We must try to live!

He took a long pull on his cigarette. He didn't know what his next painting would look like. He only knew that this series was coming to an end. He thought about the old lady in the hospital. He would go and see her tomorrow. The streets accompanied him from one lamp post to the next. He walked past hurrying commuters, taxis cruising for custom, clusters of people having a good time. He could have sat down on a café terrace, but you need to be light-hearted to sit on a terrace. He still had this great weight on his shoulders. She hadn't come. What would they have said to each other anyway? What had he been thinking? He started walking faster.

As he came through the door, the first thing he saw was the blinking red light of the answering machine. He pressed the button mechanically. An unfamiliar voice broke the silence. The words rang out. *Your grandmother – tonight – didn't suffer – personal effects*. End of message. She's not my grandmother, he thought to himself. He took a few unsteady steps over to the armchair. For some reason he didn't sit down. The resounding silence of the apartment unnerved him. The windows opposite were dark. The rectangle of the envelope was there in front of him. He picked it up. In the faint light that filtered in from the courtyard, he unsealed it and drew out the contents. It was a thick wad of pages covered in unfamiliar handwriting. The first words leapt out at him:

Mon tout amour

It was a letter. He rubbed his eyes. The light was too weak; he could hardly make out the words. He went to switch on the light then changed his mind. He lit the candle on the windowsill. In the flickering light of the flame, he sat down and began to read.

I have just learnt that I am very ill

The image of the frail old lady, the odour of the hospital, came back to him. He didn't get it. He was seized with impatience. He had to understand. He skimmed through the pages, deciphering sentences at random.

We played together that morning

His head hurt. The words were all in a muddle. He forced himself to read on, skipped ahead several pages.

To punish me your father had decided to rip you away from me

He scanned the lines feverishly. He felt like he was on the edge of a precipice. He shook off the feeling of vertigo. He picked up sentences at random.

Making plans to leave your father

I am still your mother

Blood pounded in his temples.

I am going to ask someone to deliver this letter to your grandmother

How had the old lady got hold of this document? His grandmother had died long before he was born. If Geneviève had found this at his father's house, why had she never said anything? But if his mother had died when he was three, why does she say she wanted to give this letter to his grandmother? The old lady's words rang in his ear: *I am a little like your grandmother*. How he had always loathed that sentence. A huge, dull anger swelled inside him. A loathing of other people and of himself. He wanted to vomit.

All these years

He remembered Geneviève's words: *There are things one has to do. Wait until I'm dead.* He recalled how his father used to clam up whenever he asked him. He saw him lying dead on the cement tiles. He saw his lips fixed in a rictus grin.

He saw the photograph. You were three years old; she drowned; her body was never found.

I don't think I'll be coming out of hospital again

Rage smouldered in his stomach.

I love you and I will keep searching for you until the very end

He wanted to howl. He didn't want to comprehend. The lines were cloaked in a shroud. Hands burning, he skimmed to the end. He wanted to hope.

Now that you have finished reading these pages, I want you to promise not to sit staring into the void. Don't be tempted to commune with solitude. Go out and do something impulsive, simple, consoling. Something that connects you to the world. I don't know what – have a drink with friends, cuddle your kids, lose yourself in a book, throw yourself into your work, open a good bottle of wine, drink it with your wife and tell her you love her. If I were there, I would soothe your anguished heart. I would take you in my arms. But I'm not there, so instead, let life take you in its arms. Promise me you will.

I promise I will do the same. I shall die without feeling alone or sad. Don't worry about me. Even here, in these lines, I am touching you, you are comforting me. Words, in the end, led me to you. Let me lay my love under your feet, my kisses upon your years, my thoughts all around you. Have faith. Don't shut yourself away. I want you to inherit joy, lust for life, the impulse to love. We are still alive as long as we love and are loved. I cannot bear for you to be unhappy.

At the end of the undulating line of her hand, he read these last words:

I love you and I am watching over you, my beloved boy.

He was sweating and shivering all at once.

At the bottom of the page was a final inscription. A date. His vision was blurred. He turned the sheet of paper over. Nothing more. Emptiness. Silence. The pristine page, like a murder. He went back. To the date. He said it out loud, slowly. In a stupor, he tried to work it out, to make sure, he couldn't bear to admit it: seven years. He felt himself falling like a stone into an abyss.

Seven years ago.

He couldn't believe it.

In the silence of the studio, he sounded the words out loud, emphasising each one, like a self-inflicted wound: 'My mother died seven years ago.'

He looked up. On the other side of the courtyard, the lights were still off. And yet he could see the woman, framed by her window. He saw her, that evening, as she crossed the bedroom. At last she was coming towards him. Now he saw her perfectly clearly, standing in the centre of the frame. She looked at him. He saw her face, her eyes, her smile. He felt her breath. In a movement as slow as those he had imagined a thousand times, she reached out her hand to him. He held his hand out too, towards her. It hit the glass. The woman vanished. The vision melted away. His hand fell back onto the chair. A stifled moan caught in his throat. His fingers gripped the worn leather; they squeezed harder and harder, until it hurt.

It had to end. Now. He was going to let himself slip away. Drown, like in his nightmare. Disappear. In the darkness into which he'd tumbled. He mustn't move, at all, not even the rise and fall of his chest. Must stop breathing.

But despite himself, the world that until then had

been standing stock still, the indifferent world, began to turn again. He could hear again, feel again. The sighs, tremors and creaks of his surroundings, the pangs, jolts and aches of his body, heat and cold, emptiness and plenitude, shadow and light, everything was reborn. It all reappeared around him and inside him. So fast, so violently, that if he hadn't been sitting down already he would have collapsed. Life had brought him back to earth. In his whole body, all the way to the tips of his fingers and toes, he felt the powerful vibrations of the explosion that had just occurred, the deafening sound of a massive door slamming shut. Coming back to life, with its stifling blows. Rage and impotence collided in him with a roar. His muscles tensed. He felt like a fight, but against what, against whom? The pages were burning his hands. He retched, then abruptly stood up.

The envelope slid to the ground. Something slipped out of it. It was a postcard. He stared at it blindly, until eventually, mechanically, he bent down to pick it up. There was nothing written on the back. He turned it over. He saw the couple, the room, the mirror.

He looked up. The lights opposite had come on.

The woman was at home. She'd come back, she was really there. In the turmoil of his emotions, a weariness prevented him from feeling anything. The woman who had so intrigued him was now so real and ordinary that he couldn't think why he used to watch her all the time. She was standing by the window. He didn't move. She glanced in his direction and then, in one swift movement, drew the curtains closed.

He was dead.

He was lost.

He couldn't think.

The doorbell broke the silence.

His hand was still clutching the letter.

He couldn't move.

He stood, rooted to the spot.

He thought he was dreaming.

The bell rang again, for a long time.

It was only then, astonished he could still walk, that he went over to open the door.

Ariane was standing there.

She moved towards him, rose onto her toes, cupped his face in her hands and tenderly kissed him.

Lines from Paul Valéry's *The Graveyard by the Sea*, are translated by David Pollard https://intranslation. brooklynrail.org/french/the-graveyard-by-the-sea/

The line on page 128 (The wind is rising! ... We must try to live!) is taken from the translation by C. Day Lewis https://allpoetry.com/The-Graveyard-By-The-Sea

The quotation on page 72 is from *The Bell Jar*, by Sylvia Plath

• This first English-language edition published by Les Fugitives in the United Kingdom in June 2022 • Les Fugitives Ltd, 91 Cholmley Gardens, Fortune Green Road, West Hampstead, London NW6 1UN • www. lesfugitives.com • Originally published as *Les cœurs inquiets* © Gallimard, 2020 • English-language translation © Natasha Lehrer, 2022 • Cover artwork © Anaïs Mims • Cover design by Sarah Schulte • Text design and typesetting by MacGuru Ltd • All rights reserved • No part of this publication may be reproduced, stored in a retrieval system or transmitted in any form or by any means, electronic, mechanical, photocopying, recording or otherwise, without prior permission in writing from Les Fugitives editions • A CIP catalogue record for this book is available from the British Library • The rights of Lucie Paye and Natasha Lehrer to be identified respectively as author and translator of this work have been identified in accordance with Section 77 of the Copyright, Designs and Patents Act 1988 • Printed in the UK by the CPI Group, UK • ISBN 978-1-7397783-1-6 • This book is supported by the Institut français (Royaume-Uni) as part of the Burgess programme, by the Centre National du Livre, and by The Jan Michalski Foundation •

Founded in 2014, Les Fugitives is an independent press publishing contemporary literary fiction and narrative non-fiction in translation from the French, as well as modern classics and contemporary English originals in 'the quick brown fox' collection.

In *the quick brown fox*:

No. 91/92: notes on a Parisian commute
by **Lauren Elkin**

We Still Have the Telephone
by **Erica Van Horn**

In translation from the French:

The Child Who
by **Jeanne Benameur**
trans. Bill Johnston

Eve out of Her Ruins and *The Living Days*
by **Ananda Devi**
trans. Jeffrey Zuckerman

This Tilting World
by **Colette Fellous**
trans. Sophie Lewis

Now, Now, Louison and *Nativity*
by **Jean Frémon**
trans. Cole Swensen

Translation as Transhumance
by **Mireille Gansel**
trans. Ros Schwartz

A Respectable Occupation
by **Julia Kerninon**
trans. Ruth Diver

Little Dancer Aged Fourteen
by **Camille Laurens**
trans. Willard Wood

Blue Self-Portrait and *Poetics of Work*
by **Noémi Lefebvre**
trans. Sophie Lewis

Suite for Barbara Loden and *The White Dress*
by **Nathalie Léger**
trans. Natasha Lehrer and Cécile Menon

Exposition
by **Nathalie Léger**
trans. Amanda DeMarco

The Governesses and *The Fool and Other Moral Tales*
by **Anne Serre**
trans. Mark Hutchinson

Selfies
by **Sylvie Weil**
trans. Ros Schwartz

• www.lesfugitives.com •